Praise for *The Dinner List*

"A bittersweet tale of love, loss, and living with the memories."
—*Kirkus Reviews*

"This fun book will make readers reflect on friendship and lost love and how we remember the past." —*Real Simple*

"Themes of love, loss, and forgiveness weave through this intriguing mix of the real and the fanciful." —*Booklist*

"A fun meandering through time that also touches profoundly on the many different types of love we feel for others." —*Betches*

"*The Dinner List* offers a menu of keen-eyed, compassionate insights about the relationships that nourish us." —*Shelf Awareness*

"Charming, magical read." —*Hello Giggles*

"Imagine that you could gather the people you've loved—dead or alive—at one table, for one night, with a chance to heal yourself once and for all. *The Dinner List* is a heartbreakingly romantic book framed by such an evening. It's Serle's unflinching investigation into the triumph and failings of love that makes this book one of a kind. A touch magic, a touch tragic, and absolutely compelling from beginning to end." —Stephanie Danler, *New York Times* bestselling author of *Sweetbitter*

The Dinner List

ALSO BY REBECCA SERLE

When You Were Mine
The Edge of Falling
Famous in Love
Truly Madly Famously

The Dinner List

REBECCA SERLE

FLATIRON
BOOKS
NEW YORK

THE DINNER LIST. Copyright © 2018 by Rebecca Serle. All rights reserved. Printed in the United States of America. For information, address Flatiron Books, 175 Fifth Avenue, New York, N.Y. 10010.

www.flatironbooks.com

Designed by Devan Norman

The Library of Congress has cataloged the hardcover edition as follows:

Names: Serle, Rebecca, author.
Title: The dinner list / Rebecca Serle.
Description: First edition. | New York : Flatiron Books, 2018.
Identifiers: LCCN 2018019807| ISBN 9781250295187 (hardcover) |
    ISBN 9781250315830 (international, sold outside the U.S., subject to rights
    availability) | ISBN 9781250295200 (ebook)
Subjects: | GSAFD: Love stories.
Classification: LCC PS3619.E748 D56 2018 | DDC 813/ .6—dc23
LC record available at https://lccn.loc.gov/2018019807

ISBN 978-1-250-29519-4 (trade paperback)

Our books may be purchased in bulk for promotional, educational, or business use. Please contact your local bookseller or the Macmillan Corporate and Premium Sales Department at 1-800-221-7945, extension 5442, or by email at MacmillanSpecialMarkets@macmillan.com.

First Flatiron Books Paperback Edition: June 2019

10 9 8 7 6 5 4

For my grandmother Sylvia Pesin,
who taught me that first, baby,
you gotta love yourself.

And for her Sam—the first person on my list.

How many miles to Babylon?
Three score miles and ten—
Can I get there by candlelight?
Yes, and back again—
If your feet are nimble and light
You can get there by candlelight.

—TRADITIONAL NURSERY RHYME

The stars you see at night are the
unblinking eyes of sleeping elephants,
who sleep with one eye open
to best keep watch over us.

—GREGORY COLBERT,
Ashes and Snow

7:30 P.M.

W E'VE BEEN WAITING FOR AN HOUR." That's what Audrey says. She states it with a little bit of an edge, her words just bordering on cursive. That's the thing I think first. Not *Audrey Hepburn is at my birthday dinner* but *Audrey Hepburn is annoyed.*

Her hair is longer than the image I've always held of her in my mind. She's wearing what looks to be a pantsuit, but her legs are hidden under the table, so it's hard to tell. Her top is black, with a crème-colored collar, three round buttons down the front. A cardigan is looped over the back of her chair.

I step back. I take them in. All of them. They're seated at a round table, right in the center of the restaurant. Audrey is facing the door, Professor Conrad to her right and Robert to her left. Tobias sits on the other side of Robert, to his left is Jessica, and in between her and Tobias is my empty chair.

"We started without you, Sabrina," Conrad says, holding up his wineglass. He's drinking a deep red; so is Jessica. Audrey has a scotch, neat; Tobias has a beer; Robert has nothing.

"Are you going to sit?" Tobias asks me. His voice cracks a little at the edges, and I think that he's still smoking.

"I don't know," I say. I'm surprised I have the ability for words, because this is insane. Maybe I'm dreaming. Maybe this is some sort of mental breakdown. I blink. I think maybe when I open my eyes it will be just Jessica seated there, which is what I'd been expecting. I have the urge to bolt out the door, or maybe go to the bathroom, splash some cold water on my face to determine whether or not they're really here—whether we're all really here together.

"Please," he says. There is a hint of desperation in his voice.

Please. Before he left, that was the word I used. *Please.* It didn't make a difference then.

I think about it. Because I do not know what else to do. Because Conrad is pouring Merlot from the bottle and because I can't just keep standing here.

"This is freaking me out," I say. "What's going on?"

"It's your birthday," Audrey says.

"I love this restaurant," Conrad says. "Hasn't changed in twenty-five years."

"You knew I'd be here," Jessica says. "We'll just make room for a few more." I wonder what she said when she got here. Whether she was surprised or delighted.

"Perhaps we could talk," Robert says.

Tobias says nothing. That was always our problem. He was so willing to allow silence to speak for him. The frustration I feel at him next to me overwhelms my disbelief in my situation. I sit.

The restaurant bustles around us, the diners undisturbed by what's going on here. A father tries to quiet a small child; a waiter pours wine into glasses. The restaurant is small, maybe twelve tables total. There are red potted hydrangeas by the doorway and a soft sprinkling of holiday lights line the place where the wall meets the ceiling. It's December, after all.

"I need a drink," I declare.

Professor Conrad claps his hands together. I remember he used to do that right before class would let out or he'd assign a big project. It's his way of anticipating action. "I came all the way from California for this blessed event, so the least you could do is catch me up on what you're doing now. I don't even know what you ended up majoring in."

"You want an update on my life?" I ask.

Jessica rolls her eyes next to me. "Communications," she says.

Professor Conrad puts a hand to his chest in a show of feigned shock.

"I'm a book editor now," I say a bit defensively. "Jessica, what is going on?"

Jessica shakes her head. "This is your dinner." My list. She knows, of course. She was there when I made it. It was her idea. The five people, living or dead, you'd like to have dinner with.

"You don't think this is insane?" I say.

She takes a sip of wine. "A little. But crazy things happen every day. Haven't I always told you that?"

When we lived together, in that cramped apartment on Twenty-first Street, she had inspirational quotes everywhere. On the bathroom mirror. On the Ikea desk that held our television. Right by the door. *Worrying is wishing for what you don't want. Man plans and God laughs.*

"Is this everyone?" Robert asks.

Audrey flips over her wrist. "I'd hope so," she says.

I take a sip of wine. I take a deep breath.

"Yes," I answer. "This is everyone."

They look at me. All five of them. They look expectant, hopeful. They look like I'm supposed to tell them why they're here.

But I can't do that. Not yet, anyway. So instead, I open my menu.

"Why don't we order," I say. And we do.

ONE

I FIRST SAW TOBIAS AT AN art exhibit at the Santa Monica Pier. Four years later we exchanged names on the subway stuck underground at Fourteenth Street, and we had our first date crossing the Brooklyn Bridge. Our story spanned exactly one decade, right down to the day we ended. But as it's been said before—it's easier to see the beginnings of things, and harder to see the ends.

I was in college, my sophomore year. I was taking Conrad's philosophy class. Part of the course was a weekly field trip organized by students on a rotating basis. Someone took us to the Hollywood sign, another to an abandoned house on Mulholland designed by a famous architect I had never heard of. I'm not sure what the point was except that Conrad, self-admittedly, liked to get out of the classroom. "This is not where learning takes place," he often said.

For my outing I chose the art exhibit *Ashes and Snow*. I had heard about it from some friends who had gone the weekend before. Two giant tents were erected on the beach by the Santa Monica Pier, and the artist Gregory Colbert was showing his work—big, beautiful photographic images of human beings living in harmony with wildlife. There had been a giant billboard that sat on Sunset Boulevard the entire year of 2006—a small child reading to a kneeling elephant.

It was the week before Thanksgiving. I was flying home the next day to Philadelphia to spend the holiday with my mother's extended family. My mom was contemplating a move back East, where she was from. We'd been in California since I was six years old, since right after my father left.

I was flustered. I remember cursing myself that I'd signed up to organize this event when I had so much other stuff going on. I was fighting with Anthony—my on-again, off-again business-major boyfriend, who rarely left the confines of his fraternity house except for "around the world" parties, where the only traveling was to the toilet after mixing too many different kinds of booze. The whole relationship was fiction, comprised mainly of text messages and drunken nights that we somehow cobbled into togetherness. In truth, we were biding our time. He was two years older, a senior with a finance job in New York already lined up. I thought, loosely, we'd someday transition this playing pretend into playing house, but of course we never did.

Ashes and Snow was stunning. The indoor space was dramatic and yet serene—like practicing yoga at the very edge of a cliff.

Our student group scattered quickly—mesmerized by the scale

of the thing. A child kissing a lion, a little boy sleeping with a bob-
cat, a man swimming with whales. And then I saw him. Standing in
front of a photograph I can only recall with a pull in my heart so
strong I have to take a step back. The picture was of a little boy, eyes
closed, eagle wings spread behind him.

I was instantly in awe. Of the photographs, the image itself, and
this boy. The one outside the photograph. Brown shaggy hair. Low-
slung jeans. Two brown shirts layered like dirt. I didn't see his eyes
immediately. I didn't yet know they were the most searing shade of
green, like jewels, so sharp they could cut right through you.

I stood next to him. We didn't look at each other. For minutes.
Five, maybe more. I couldn't tell what I was seeing—him, or the boy.
But I felt a current between us; the sand kicked up around us like it
was charged, too. Everything seemed to converge. For one beautiful,
exquisite moment there was no separation.

"I've been four times already," he told me, eyes still gazing forward. "I never want to leave this spot."

"He's beautiful," I said.

"The whole exhibit is pretty incredible."

"Are you in school?" I asked.

"Mm-hm," he said. He glanced at me. "UCLA."

"USC," I told him, tapping my chest.

If he were a different kind of guy—say, Anthony—he would have
made a face. He would have talked about the rivalry. But I'm not even
sure he knew about this ritual we were supposed to engaged in—the
Trojans versus the Bruins.

"What do you study?" I asked him.

He gestured toward the canvas. "I'm a photographer," he said.

"What kind?"

"I'm not so sure yet. Right now my specialty is being mildly bad at everything."

He laughed; so did I. "I doubt that's true."

"How come?"

"I don't know," I said. I looked back at the photograph. "I just do."

A group of teenage girls hovered nearby, staring at him. When I looked over they giggled and dispersed. I couldn't blame them—he was stunning.

"What about you?" he asked. "Let me guess. Acting."

"Ha. Hardly. Communications," I said.

"I was close." He extended his pointer finger out toward my chest. I wanted to grab on to the end. "Anyway, good skill to have."

The most important thing in communication is hearing what isn't said.

"That's what my mom tells me."

He turned to me then, and his eyes opened to mine. That's the only way I know how to describe it. It was a key in a lock. The door just swung free.

The wind picked up, and my hair started flying around me. It was longer then, much longer than it is now. I tried to tame it, but it was like trying to catch a butterfly. It kept escaping my reach.

"You look like a lion," he said. "I wish I had my camera."

"It's too long," I said. I was blushing. I hoped the hair was covering it.

He just smiled at me. "I need to go," he said. "But now I don't want to."

I could see Conrad behind him, lecturing four of our group near a photograph of a giraffe that appeared to be almost to scale. Conrad waved me over. "Me too," I said. "I mean, me neither."

I wanted to say more, or I wanted him to. I stood there unmoving, waiting for him to ask for my number. Any more information. But he didn't. He just gave me a little salute and walked back toward Conrad and out of the tent. I didn't even get his name.

Jessica was home when I got back to our dorm. We were two of the only sophomores on the entirety of USC's campus who still lived in university housing. But it came out to be cheaper, and neither one of us could afford to move. We didn't have Orange County or Hollywood money like so many of our fellow students.

Back then Jessica had long brown hair and big glasses and she wore long flowy dresses nearly every day, even in winter. Although the coldest it ever got was in the fifties.

"How was the exhibit?" she asked. "Do you want to go to Pi Kapp tonight? Sumir said they're throwing a beach-themed party but we don't have to dress up."

I tossed my bag down and slumped in the living room chair. There wasn't room for a couch. Jessica was on the floor.

"Maybe," I said.

"Call Anthony," she said, getting up to turn off the ringing teakettle.

"I don't think I want to be with him anymore," I said.

I could hear her pouring the hot water, ripping open a teabag. "What do you mean you *think*?"

I picked at the hem of my denim shorts. "There was this guy at the exhibit today."

Jessica came back holding a steaming cup. She offered me some. I shook my head. "Tell me," she said. "From class?"

"No, he was just there."

"What's his deal?"

"He's a photographer; he goes to UCLA."

Jessica blew on her tea and settled back down on the floor. "So are you going to see him?"

"No," I said. "I don't even know his name."

Jessica frowned at me. She'd had exactly one boyfriend in her entire life—Sumir Bedi, the man who would a few years later become her husband. Their relationship didn't strike me as being particularly romantic; it still doesn't. They were both in the same dorm freshman year. He asked her to his fraternity invite, she said yes, and they started dating. They slept together a year later. It was both of their first times. She didn't talk about him and get mushy, but they also rarely fought. I suspected it was because neither one of them drank much. She was a romantic person, though, and deeply invested in my love life. She wanted every detail. Sometimes I found myself embellishing just to give her something more to hear.

"I just don't think I want to be with Anthony anymore." How could I explain what had happened? That in a moment I'd given my heart to a stranger I'd probably never see again?

She set her teacup down on the coffee table. "All right," she said. "We'll just have to find this guy."

My heart bloomed with affection for her. That was Jessica—she didn't need a way, just a why. "You're crazy," I told her. I stood up and glanced out our twentieth-story window. Outside students were walking back and forth across campus like tiny tin soldiers sent on a mission. It all looked so orderly and intentional from up here. "He doesn't even go USC. It's impossible."

"Have a little faith," she told me. "I think your problem is you don't believe in fate."

Jessica came from a conservative family in Michigan. I would watch her evolution slowly, from Christian Midwesterner to full-blown liberal hippie, and then—many years later—a sharp right into East Coast conservative.

The week before she had come home with a stack of magazines, paper, and colored pencils. "We're making dream boards," she had announced.

I looked at the supplies and turned back to my book. "No thanks."

Jessica had been taking this course in spirituality—some kind of "Unleash the Power Within" Tony Robbins stepchild led by a woman with a self-ascribed Hindu name.

"You haven't done a single exercise with me," Jessica had said, plopping herself down onto a pillow on our floor.

I surveyed her. "You have anything with a little less glitter?"

Her eyes brightened. "Swani asked us to make a list of the five people living or dead we'd like to have dinner with." She rummaged in her supply bag and pulled out a stack of yellow Post-its. "No glitter."

"Will this make you happy?" I asked, closing my book, already resigned.

"For about an hour," she said, but I could see the spark in her eye. I never said yes to stuff like this, even though she always kept asking.

She started talking a lot then. About the exercise, about what it meant, about how the imagined fictional dinner was like a reckoning between parts of yourself you needed to come to terms with—yadda yadda. I wasn't really listening; I just started drafting.

The first few were easy: Audrey Hepburn, because I was a nineteen-year-old girl. Plato, because I had read *The Republic* four times since high school and was riveted—and because Professor Conrad spoke of his contributions often. I wrote Robert's name down without even thinking. As soon as I saw it I wanted to cross it out, but I didn't. He was still my father, even if I could barely remember ever knowing him.

Two more.

I loved my mom's mom. Her name was Sylvia, and she had passed away the year before. I missed her. I wrote her name down. I couldn't think of a fifth.

I looked over at Jessica, intently making a list on a giant piece of parchment paper in red and gold pencil.

I handed the note to her. She looked it over, nodded, and handed it back to me. I stuck it in my pocket and went back to my book. She seemed placated.

But now, about Tobias, she was not. "I do believe in fate," I told her. I hadn't, but I did now. It was hard to explain. How big ideas about life and love had solidified in ten minutes of standing next to him. "I shouldn't have said anything. It was stupid. It was a moment."

But it was a moment I wanted to make more of, and we went looking. We couldn't find him online (searching "green eyes" and "UCLA" on Facebook did not give us very positive results—and something told me he wasn't the sort of guy who had a profile), so we drove up to the UCLA campus in Sumir's Toyota Corolla, which wouldn't go more than forty on the freeway.

"What's your plan when we get there?" I asked Jessica. "Start yelling 'boy with brown hair' loudly?"

"Relax," she told me. "*I'm* not yelling anything."

She parked in Westwood and we walked to the north side of campus, where the row houses and student apartments were. They all sat on tree-lined streets that poured out onto Sunset and up into the impeccable hills of Bel Air. I followed behind, grateful that it was a sunny day, there were a lot of people around, and we were blending in well.

"I know we're not supposed to say this," I said. "But UCLA is way nicer than USC."

"In location only," Jessica said. She stopped in front of a bulletin board posted outside a campus building—library? I wasn't sure.

"Aha," she said. "As I'd hoped."

I peered closer. It was a club board. The Food Club, Poetry Club. I followed Jessica's finger. It tapped a yellow flyer lightly. "The Photography Club," I read.

Jessica beamed. "You're welcome."

"I'm impressed," I said. "But this doesn't mean anything. He probably doesn't belong to it. He didn't really seem like a club kind of a guy. And what would we do, crash their meeting?"

Jessica rolled her eyes. "As charming as I find your negativity, they're holding an open house next Tuesday, so you can just go to that."

I shook my head. "If he was there, I'd seem crazy."

Jessica shrugged. "Or you'd live happily ever after."

"Right," I said. "One of the two." But I felt excitement spring a leak in me. What if I saw him again? What would I say?

My stomach growled then.

"Want to go to In-N-Out?" Jessica asked.

"Definitely."

We started to wander back to the Corolla, but before we did I snatched the flyer and stuffed it into my bag.

"I saw nothing," Jessica said, looping her arm through mine.

When we got home I took out the Post-it and added a fifth. *Him*.

7:45 P.M.

D OES ANYONE ELSE LIKE CARP?" Conrad is asking. We haven't ordered yet because no one can agree on what to do. Conrad is determined to share, Robert wants to order separately, Audrey is displeased with the menu, and Jessica and Tobias have eaten two breadbaskets already. It irritates me that he has an appetite.

"I'm still breastfeeding," Jessica says to no one in particular. "I need the carbs."

The waiter comes over for the second time and I just jump in. "I'll have the frisée salad and the risotto," I say. I send Conrad a look. He nods.

"The scallops," he says. "And some of those aphrodisiacs."

The waiter looks confused. He opens his mouth and closes it again.

"Oysters," Audrey clarifies wearily. "I'll have the same, with the frisée salad."

Professor Conrad elbows her. "Audrey, I never," he says.

She isn't having it. She's still irritated.

It strikes me as everyone places their orders—pasta and soup for Jessica, steak and salad for Robert—that I didn't really think this through. When I chose each of these five people to be on my list, it was entirely about me. My issues with each of them, and my mixed desires to be in their presence. I didn't think of how they'd get along *together.*

I permit myself a glance to my left, to Tobias. I already know what he'll order. I knew it the instant I opened the menu. I do this sometimes, now, when I'm at a restaurant. I'll scan the menu and choose what he would want. I know he'll get the burger and fries, extra mustard. And the beet salad. Tobias loves beets. He was a vegetarian for a while, but it didn't stick.

"The crudo and the scallops," he says.

I whip my head to look at him. He raises his shoulders up back at me. "The burger looked good, too," he says. "But I just ate all that bread."

Tobias was concerned about his health in odd ways. Sometimes I thought he had a thing for staying thin—maybe because it made him look like a starving artist? He didn't work out, he wasn't a runner, but he'd skip meals sometimes or he'd come home with a new juicer and declare he didn't want to eat processed foods anymore. He was an excellent cook. The crudo. I should have figured.

The waiter takes our menus and then Audrey leans forward. For the first time I catch small little lines around her eyes. She must be in her late forties.

"I came with some conversation topics," she tells me. She speaks in that low, hushed voice we all know so well. She's delicate, so feminine it pains, and I have a pang of regret that she is seated at this table with us. She shouldn't be here; it's not worth her time.

"We don't need topics," Conrad says, brushing her off. "We just need wine and a theme."

"A theme?" asks Robert. He looks up from his water. He's a small man, short. Even seated you can tell. My mother had two inches on him. I always thought I fell somewhere in the middle based on the small pile of old photographs, but looking at him now I know I'm all his.

We have the same green eyes, the same long nose, the same crooked smile and reddish-brownish curly hair. He didn't go to college. No one in his family did either. He got tuberculosis when he was nineteen and spent a year and a half in a hospital. Solitary confinement. His own mother could only visit through a glass wall.

My mom told me that story years later. Years after he had left, after he was already dead and I couldn't ask him any follow-up questions myself. I never knew whether it was supposed to humanize him, or make him seem more obtuse, abstract—untouchable. But I also never knew if she kept on loving him. I still don't.

"Theme!" Conrad calls. "Let's have a theme."

"Global service," Audrey says.

Conrad nods. He takes a notebook and pen out of his breast pocket. He always kept a notebook there, should he be inspired. He used to take it out periodically during class and scribble things inside.

"Julie!" Conrad says. "You're up."

Jessica looks at him, a piece of baguette in her mouth. "It's *Jessica*," she says.

"Jessica, of course."

"*Family,*" she says, sighing. "But I don't think this is the point."

"Responsibility," Robert adds. I do an inadequate job of choking back a laugh. Responsibility. How ridiculous.

Then Tobias. He sits back in his chair. He loops his hands behind his head. "Love," he says. He says it so simply, so easily. Like it's obvious. Like it's the only possible answer to Conrad's question.

But it isn't, of course. Because if it was I wouldn't need him at this dinner. If that were true, we'd still be together.

I clear my throat. "History," I say, as if to counter.

Conrad nods. Audrey sips. Jessica balks.

"We've been over this," she says, glaring at Tobias and me. "You guys can't keep living in the past."

Let go and let God.

"Sometimes it is impossible to move forward without understanding what happened." Conrad.

"What did happen?" Audrey says.

I keep my eyes on the table, but I still feel his on me. I wish he were seated where Conrad is. I wish I couldn't smell him—heady and dense—or find his foot under the table, so close that if I wanted to I could hold it against mine.

"Everything," I say after a moment. "Everything happened."

"Well," Conrad says. "Let's start there."

TWO

THE TUESDAY AFTER OUR UCLA INVESTIGATION, I was in Professor Conrad's office trying to argue my way up to a C-plus for a written exam I had completely tanked. I was always doing terribly in his class. I couldn't quite get there. Not that I was trying that hard. Admittedly, I had let all my grades slip. I had no good reason besides the fact that I was tired of school, of homework and lectures and tests. I didn't want to do it anymore. And the ongoing drama with Anthony wasn't helping things.

"Maybe you're in the wrong major," Jessica told me, but it was too late to change. If I did, I'd be there for another three years, and that wasn't an option—financially or any way else.

"You've gotten used to the idea that outcomes are irrelevant," Conrad said. "In my class, I do not believe that's true."

"Please." I was close to tears. "Can I do extra credit?"

Conrad shook his head. "I don't offer extra credit."

"I can't get a D."

"You can," he said. "Matter of fact, you did."

Fear coiled in my stomach. "I'm sorry," I mumbled.

Conrad put a hand on my shoulder. It felt fatherly. I was unaccustomed. "You can do better on the next one and raise your average up," he told me. "This is not your final ticket."

I gathered up my things and left his office—entitled, annoyed, angry. I checked my watch. If I left now I could make it to UCLA's campus by seven. The crumbled piece of yellow paper at the bottom of my book bag informed me that the photography open house wasn't until seven.

I called Jessica. "I have to study," she said. "But Sumir is in class and I have his car keys here waiting for you."

"Meet me downstairs."

There was traffic on the 405. I sat and flipped between 98.7 and NPR. They were doing some special on NASA protocol. They had someone on who had just returned from a space tour. "The thing that struck me the most," he said, "was how in some capacity of measurement the universe is actually finite. How do we possibly wrap our heads around the end of the end?"

I changed the radio back to Britney Spears.

The flyer said the show was going to be in the Billy Wilder Theater. I asked directions from a security guard when I got to UCLA and after a few wrong turns managed to find a parking spot on the street. My watch read 6:57 P.M. Just in time.

My heart started to pump as I took the sidewalk and then steps leading to the theater. What if he was actually there? What would I say? How would I explain my presence? Act surprised. *A friend told me to come.* That wasn't strictly untrue. He might not even recognize me.

I found a lip gloss in my bag. I swiped it across, took a deep breath, and pulled the door open.

The show was set up onstage. Photographs hung from partition boards and people in the aisles held plastic cups filled with red wine. I made my way closer to the stage. So far, no him.

"Are you one of the artists?" a girl with a long braid said. She had on bell-bottom jeans and a peasant blouse I recognized from Forever 21. Jessica had tried on the same one at the Beverly Center last weekend.

It felt like she was onto me. "No," I said. "No, just looking."

She nodded, took a sip of wine.

"You?"

"That's my stuff up there." She gestured to a partition wall on the far left-hand side of the stage. I saw color. Tons of it.

"Mind if I go check it out?"

"Just as long as you don't ask me to come with you. My stuff works better if I don't speak for it."

I left her and moved up onto the stage. I took a quick scan. Nowhere. Not in the aisles, either. The crowd wasn't big, maybe thirty people in all. I thought about leaving, but I could see my new friend's eyes on me, and so I decided to go over to her work.

But something caught my eye on the way over. It was a photograph of a man. He looked tribal. Moroccan, maybe. It was from the torso up and he was smoking a cigar, mid exhale. His eyes were wide open and gray and the lines on his face were like tally marks of chalk on a board.

I knew it was his. I don't know how, but I did.

"Excuse me," I asked a kid in low-slung jeans and a baseball hat who was standing next to the board. "Whose work is this?"

He shrugged and then pointed to a plaque midway down the wall. TOBIAS SALTMAN. Next to a photo of the guy from *Ashes and Snow*. I was right.

I could feel the blood pumping through the veins in my neck. "Is he here?" I asked.

He squinted at me. "Don't think so," he said.

"Is there someone who would know?"

He peered down into the aisles and cocked his head in the direction of the girl I had just spoken to. "Ask his girlfriend," he said.

Heat. That's what I felt. Embarrassment and shame. Of course he had a girlfriend. It was obvious, and stupid to think he didn't. I wanted to take off as soon as possible.

But then I saw a number by the photograph of the man: $75. It was for sale.

I didn't have seventy-five dollars. There were only forty-nine in my checking account and maybe two hundred in savings.

But I knew I had to buy it anyway. He was already mine.

I fumbled in my bag for my checkbook. By some stroke of luck, I had it on me.

"How do I buy a photograph?" I asked a girl standing beside a photo display of sunflowers. "Can I use a check?"

"Jenkins will help you." She gestured toward a young woman in jeans and a brocade top, pixie cut, leaning against the far wall and talking wildly with her hands. I went over.

"I'd like to buy that photograph," I said, pointing at Tobias's piece.

She unhinged herself from the wall. "You got it," she said. "His work is pretty great, huh?"

I nodded.

"I think this might be his first sale. Too bad the kid isn't here."

I wrote her a check, determined to somehow put the money needed into the account so it wouldn't bounce, and she wrapped it for me—brown paper and string, no tape. "Shit," she said. "I forgot to buy some. This is our first sale."

I waved to his girlfriend on the way out. She smiled. She had a gap between her two front teeth. It made my affection for him grow even greater.

I put the photo on the passenger seat on the drive home. When I got back to the apartment, Jessica was out. I knew I wouldn't hang it up. Later, when she asked, I told her he hadn't been there, he must not belong.

"At least you tried," she said.

I kept the photograph under my bed wrapped in the brown paper for the next two years. Sometimes at night I would sneak it out of its foldings and hold it in my hands like something I had stolen.

7:52 P.M.

H ISTORY," CONRAD SAYS, TAPPING HIS PEN against the table. "It's an interesting choice."

"I was a history teacher," Robert says.

"Seriously?" I say.

Robert fixes his gaze on his water glass. "For ten years," he says.

Conrad claps his hands together. "Wonderful!" he says. "Jump on in. You can get us started."

"We should choose a focus," Audrey says. "What era? American? European? This is far too wide."

"Personal," Tobias says next to me. It feels like the first thing he's said since we sat down, even though I know it's not; we went over the crudo, and then there was love.

I close my eyes. I open them. One thing at a time. "Where?" I ask Robert.

24

"Sherman Oaks," he says.

"California."

He nods. "My wife—"

"No." I cut him off. I don't want to hear about his wife. Or his kids. Or his other life.

"We were in Fresno," I say. "Mom only moved back to Philly ten years ago. All that time . . ."

"I didn't know," Robert says.

"Yes," I say. "And yet you never thought to come back, to check on us, to even ask? You never thought maybe you owed us some of your newfound good fortune?"

Audrey smiles and leans forward. "Friends," she says. "Let's keep it civil."

"Why?" I ask. My eyes are fired up, but when they land on her soft, brown ones I find myself melting backward.

"Because we haven't even gotten our starters yet," she quips. "And no one is going anywhere."

"I didn't know you'd died until six months after," I say. "*Six* months."

"I got what I deserved," he says.

"Don't say that," Tobias interjects. He's staring at Robert with a mixture of benevolence and some kind of intensity I can't place, and I realize, like so many times before, I don't know what he means. Whether he's being sympathetic or challenging.

"Look," Jessica says. "Food."

Three waiters appear with our starters. I instantly regret the salad. It looks like a piece of modern art. Sprigs of microgreens intercepting shavings of Parmesan. I wonder if Tobias will give me some of his crudo. He used to do that—put food on my plate without my asking.

"I would very much like to explain what happened," Robert says when everyone's starter has been set down.

"We're still in history," Conrad says. "I think that would be fine."

I look across the table at him, and he raises his eyebrows at me. "What?" he says. "Is this all to talk about the weather?"

I shake my head. It's not a yes or no—more like a giving in.

"Go ahead," Audrey says. "We're all listening."

"I never had the chance to say good-bye," he starts. "She kicked me out. Your mother never wanted me to come back."

"You were a drunk," I say.

I lift a sprig of greenery off my plate and put it in my mouth. It tastes like sand.

"I was," he says. "Marcie wanted to have another baby. She wanted this whole life I couldn't give her."

"So you went and gave it to someone else?"

"I got help," Robert says.

"That's good," Conrad interjects. "A man should be marked by his ability to grow."

Life is growth. If we stop growing, we are as good as dead.

"Not all change is growth," Audrey says. I look up at her. I feel like thanking her.

"I disagree." This from Tobias. "The mere act of taking a chance, of *changing*, is by definition an act of evolution. And when we evolve, we grow. And that's the point."

"Of what?" I ask.

"Human existence," Jessica says next to me. She spoons some tomato bisque into her mouth and then waves her hand back and forth across her lips in reaction to its heat.

26

I give her a weary look. Sometimes I wish she would just, no questions asked, be on my side.

"I'm not saying what I did was right," Robert says. "But it was necessary. It was the only course of action. I had to leave."

"Necessity," Conrad repeats, but that's it.

"I was five years old," I say.

"I had to get help. I couldn't change in the present circumstance. It wasn't your mother's fault. It just . . . didn't work."

"And later?" I asked. "What about then? Why didn't you ever come back once you got better?"

"Because," he says. "I met her. And then I was afraid."

No one asks of what. We know. Losing the new life. Losing health. Losing *her*. Everything he had already lost didn't factor in.

"It's going to take more than one dinner," I say.

"But Sabrina," Robert says, looking directly at me for the first time since we sat down. "One dinner is all we've got."

THREE

W E WERE STUCK IN THE SUBWAY underground. I've had a
terrifying fear of small spaces since I was five years old,
when I was locked in the cabinet under the sink. It was a babysitting-
gone-wrong situation. Not her fault, just a game of hide-and-seek and
a jammed door. It only happened once, but once was enough.

I was employing the tools I have. Breathe deep. Do not block your
airway. Sit up straight. Keep your mind in check. Focus your breath.
Understand that it is only a feeling and that you are safe and secure.

This too shall pass.

"Are you okay?"

There were only four people in our car. Thank God. Even though
it was early and I hadn't yet picked up my morning coffee, I had noticed him when I got on. I nearly dropped my tote bag. At first I
thought it couldn't be, but there was no mistaking him. His shaggy

hair, ripped jeans, and scruffy chin. It had been four years since *Ashes and Snow* in Los Angeles, and now here we were on the other side of the country in New York, and it felt like I had finally arrived at the other point of a straight line.

Life in New York wasn't all that bad. I was living with Jessica, and our college cohorts David and Ellie were there, too. David, now a banker, was always dating older, powerful, unavailable men. He was one of only three black men in his class at Goldman, which he said gave him an advantage. I'd never seen David not excel or get what he wanted—and the men of the city were no exception. Then there was Ellie, who was perpetually single and worked on the publicity scene for a popular jewelry designer. We went out with them often, to off-off-Broadway plays that were usually shitty but cost only twenty bucks. I had a degree. I was working as an assistant for a fashion designer who was planning a big comeback. She hadn't been relevant since the late nineties, but she was launching a new line of swimwear that was putting her back on the map.

She would hit it big a year after I left, my timing always spectacular, but at that moment, heading uptown, we were working in the back of a cramped storefront. I wasn't looking forward to spending the next eight hours in sweaty darkness.

But I also didn't want to spend my day underground.

"I'm all right," I said.

I looked up at him, expecting recognition, but nothing registered on his face. He was leaning against one of the metal poles.

"The average time for a train to be stuck is three minutes and thirty-five seconds." He took out his cell phone. "I think you have about two left. Can you make it to two?"

I couldn't tell whether he was being sarcastic or not. This was often a problem of ours. I wanted sincerity, just not the way he gave it. Not with that much honesty.

I shrugged and gestured to the empty plastic seat beside me. I always figured when I saw him again, he'd know it, too. He'd say, *It's you*, and that would be that.

He sat down. "Do you live here?" he asked.

"Not specifically," I said. His face was blank. "I mean I live in Chelsea." I gestured absently toward the outside—whatever tunnel we were currently pinned to.

"Chelsea," he repeated, like the word was foreign. *Saffron. Indonesia.*

"You?"

"Williamsburg," he said.

"Sure." That seemed exactly right. We'd have a lot of arguments over the years about Brooklyn versus Manhattan. It was my feeling that I hadn't moved all the way here to live outside the city, especially back then, but for Tobias Brooklyn *was* the city. The only reason he was even on the subway that day, underground on Manhattan soil, was that he had just come from an interview at a gallery and was now headed uptown to go to a photography exhibit at the Whitney.

"Which one?" I asked when he told me. I knew the Chelsea gallery scene. Since I'd heard about Robert's death, the year before, I had taken to wandering around our neighborhood. It was a thing I did to clear my head. Not that his death should have changed anything—I hadn't seen him since I was a child—but it did, somehow. Just knowing the chance had been taken away for good.

I'd have dinner at the Empire Diner and stroll down Tenth Avenue, up and down the Twenties, popping into whatever gallery was having an opening. It was a great place to get free wine.

"Red Roof," he said.

"I hate that place." I don't know why I said it. The words just came out. Not that it wasn't true; I did hate that place. They were always showing experimental art that seemed hyperbolically obvious and simplistic. Nudes made out of candy wrappers. The demise of society at the hands of pop culture. *Sugar rot.*

"That's awesome," he said. "Me too." And then he smiled and we looked at each other and some coin fell into the slot machine deep inside me. The whole thing got set into motion. I would later look back on that moment and wonder what would have happened if I had lied. If I had told him I knew the gallery and liked it. I'm not sure we'd have been together.

"So why are you applying?"

He shrugged, leaned his head back on the glass window. "It's a job," he said.

"You're an artist." I knew this, of course, already.

"Yeah," he said. "I scream 'starving,' or something?" I guess it wasn't a tough thing to intuit. "What's your name?" he asked me, his head snapping back.

My chest rose then. It expanded so much that I no longer remembered we were underground. There was something about the exchange of a name that made me think—*know*—that this time would be the start of something.

"Sabrina," I said.

"Like the witch?"

"Ha. No. Like the mo—"

The train gave a jolt. We started moving again. I was actually disappointed. We were just getting somewhere. But when the train stopped at Forty-second Street he offered me his hand. "Want to get some coffee?" he asked.

"I'm late for work." I wanted a real date, and we were running out of time. "Here." I took out a pen. I flipped over his hand. I wrote my number. The doors closed on him. He pressed his palm up against the glass. *Don't smudge*, I thought.

He called the next day, and when he did, it was on. It was like I had taken those four years to prepare, and once that time was over, that time of tidying up, sweeping away, clearing, there was all this space. We rushed right in. We filled it up until it was bursting.

8:00 P.M.

W E'RE EATING OUR APPETIZERS IN SILENCE. Jessica keeps spearing my plate with her fork—one habit of hers, of having her around, which I do not miss. Jessica has this knack for always wanting what is on my plate—formed in the trenches of freshman-year cafeterias.

When we lived together, I'd always end up buying enough of whatever I got so we could both eat. Her husband does it now, too. I'm not sure she's even set foot in a grocery store.

"And your wife?" Audrey asks. "How did you meet her?"

"In rehab," Robert says, nervously glancing at me. "She's sober as well."

Audrey takes a sip of her drink.

I angle my plate closer to Jessica as my mind resets on what Robert

33

has just said. About how he left, met a girl in rehab, and started a new life. All things I knew, but have never heard from him, from the source.

"We understood each other," he said. "I don't know how I would live with someone who didn't know what it was like to be an addict."

Tobias nods, and I suddenly get the familiar, intense urge to hit him. He was always doing this when we were together—being casually tolerant of things that bothered me, maybe even hurt me.

"Your problem," he'd tell me, "is that you're too judgmental." As if that was supposed to be profound. As if that wasn't just an insult.

"I understand that," Audrey says. "I was never much for drugs, but I saw it take many people around me. Pity. I think it had much to do with a lack of companionship."

Companionship. *Let me sit with you in silence. Let me hold your hand and understand.*

"Do you have children?" Audrey continues. She picks up an oyster and drops a dollop of horseradish on it.

"Three girls," Robert says. "Sabrina, of course, Daisy, and Alexandra."

"Alexandra," Audrey repeats dreamily.

"Seventeen and twenty-four. The little one likes to sing. The older one . . ." Robert's voice trails off, and then he shakes his head and chuckles. I feel something pull so tight in my chest I'm afraid it's going to snap.

Conrad, it seems, is the only one who notices. "That is not much by way of an apology," he says. He takes a deep sip of wine and then sits back.

"No," Robert says. "It's not."

"I don't want an apology," I say. "There isn't anything you could say that could make up for it anyway."

"Why was I on the list?" he asks. He asks it so suddenly I'm tempted to answer honestly.

I'd put him on before he died. I left him on because I wanted to know. Because I have the same question he does: *Why?*

"She wants you to try," Jessica says, almost desperately.

"Aha," Conrad says. "Family." He looks at Jessica. She gulps some water. "Astute contribution."

She swallows. "Thank you."

"You missed all the stories, every memory," I say. "You missed everything."

"Yes." Robert shuffles his lips. I have a flash—déjà vu—of the same mannerism. Pot of coffee on the counter. Some breakfast morning among bills and cartoons. "Did your mother ever tell you how we got you home from the hospital on the night you were born?"

I shrug. "I don't know. I don't remember. Probably."

"Go on," Conrad says. "We're listening." He gestures him on with his hand.

"It was snowing," Robert says.

"Lovely," Audrey says.

"Sounds fictitious," Conrad says. "But please continue."

"It was. It was back when we lived in that little farmhouse in Pennsylvania. Do you remember that farmhouse?"

"Two chickens, one goat, three hamsters, because Sabby wanted them." This from Tobias.

Robert looks impressed. He has yet to really acknowledge Tobias. Who he is. I wonder if he knows.

"Yes. Okay. Well, we were thirty miles from the hospital."

I've heard this story from my mother. He's right. There was a storm and they had to pull over because driving conditions were so bad. My mom held me in the car and my dad went into a nearby barn to use their phone. The heat wasn't working, or they didn't have it in the car, I'm not sure. I fill the table in on this now.

"No." Robert shakes his head. "Your mother didn't stay in the car. She came inside and we spent that first night there, in the barn."

"Jesus be damned," Conrad exclaims. "Sabrina could have been the true child of God."

"You used the phone, you waited out the storm for an hour, and you drove home," I say. "That's not what happened."

"We waited out the storm all night. And there was no phone. The lines were dead."

"Why would Mom lie about that?"

Robert grazes his plate with his fork. It makes a *ch-ch-ch* sound on the ceramic. "Maybe she forgot."

I thought you were supposed to remember only the good. When I look back at my relationship with Tobias, I know I tend to do that. It's our highlights reel. Our greatest hits. The stuff that crept in, the stuff that drove us apart, I too easily forget.

"You slept on the floor with an infant?" Jessica asks. Her son, Douglas, is seven months old. Jessica is still breastfeeding. She likes to talk about it a lot. Not that I mind. Or, I should say, not that I'm not used to it. Jessica was always much more open than I am. She'd walk around our apartment topless. Bras cause cancer, apparently.

"There were blankets," Robert says. "Marcie was up all night feeding Sabrina. The farmer gave us food and drink."

"Was I born in the fourteenth century?" The vision of me, newly birthed, swaddled in burlap and lying in the arms of my adoring parents in a barn is becoming a little too much to stomach. I push some stray Parmesan toward some greens, lift the whole thing up, and chew.

"We were happy," Robert says.

"Just the one night, then," I say.

"A year," he says. "We were happy for a year."

It's true that I don't know a lot from my infancy. I guess I never asked and my mother never volunteered. I know why now, though. When someone leaves, remembering the joy is far more painful than thinking about the misery.

"Then what happened?" I ask.

"Responsibility," Audrey says. She looks a little bit sad when she says it, and I make a note to talk about her. To ask about her life. I once again feel bad for pulling her into this—my personal drama.

"It was always there," Robert says. "It got worse, not better. We fought all the time. I wasn't around as much as I should have been. She wanted me to leave."

"Not like that."

"No," he says. "Not like that."

"She remarried," Jessica says. I look at her. She shrugs. "What?" she says. "She did. And I think she's happy."

"Yeah?" Robert looks at me. He looks so hopeful it almost makes me crack.

"Doesn't make any difference," I say.

"Yes, it does," Tobias says. "It means that wasn't her only shot at happiness, and that maybe she wasn't happy, either."

"So?"

"So you can't just blame the person who leaves. If two people are unhappy, clocking the person who actually walks out the door is just getting them on a technicality."

"Convenient," I say.

Conrad clears his throat. "We're getting ahead of ourselves," he says.

"Impossible not to," Audrey says. She looks entertained now. A little bit perkier.

"Everything is happening at once," Jessica says. She puts a hand to her forehead and holds it there.

"That is true, my dear," Conrad says. "And it's all happening right now, so we may as well figure out what it is."

FOUR

H E WAS LATE. I WAS STANDING at the mouth of the Brooklyn Bridge, on the Manhattan side. This was going to be our first date. He had called and asked me if I wanted to go for a walk. And now here we were.

It was a fall day. September twenty-third. It was chilly, but not cold. I wanted to move, though. I was anxious for him to get there.

He jogged over thirty-three minutes after we had planned to meet. He came up from the Brooklyn side, a sheepish smile on his face.

"We were on opposite ends," he said. "I guess I should have specified."

He grinned at me. I grinned at him. We started walking.

The walk over the Brooklyn Bridge is spectacular anytime, but at sunset it's really something. It was like the universe had put us on opposite sides so we could walk together then, in that moment, with the sky turning from rage (red, orange) to surrender (blue, yellow) right around us.

Somewhere in the middle he slipped his hand into mine. It was thrilling.

"Tell me about you," I said.

"I'd rather hear about you," he said.

"I'm not that interesting," I said.

"Not true." He reached over with his free hand and brushed some hair out of my face. "You're the most interesting girl in the world."

I swallowed. "Well, I graduated from USC and I moved here immediately after. I live with my best friend."

"In Chelsea," he said.

"Right. In Chelsea. And I work for a crazy fashion designer."

"What do you want to do?" he asked.

"I'm not sure," I said. "I guess that's the problem." He squeezed my hand. I squeezed back. "What about you?"

"I got the job."

"Red Roof?"

He nodded. "I took it," he said, like he was confessing something.

"That's great."

"Yeah?"

"Yeah. It's a block away from my apartment."

I laughed then, embarrassed at what I had just implied. He held my hand a little bit tighter.

"Want to see a movie?" he asked me.

"Yes."

"You pick, I'll buy."

We ended up seeing a showing of *North by Northwest* at a theater in Williamsburg I had never been to where they served up independent and second-run movies on a pull-down screen along with cheap red wine and four-dollar beers.

We bent our heads together. He put his arm around me. When Cary Grant said, "Apparently the only performance that will satisfy you is when I play dead," Tobias tilted my head back and kissed me.

It wasn't a wild kiss. We'd have plenty of those. It was a benchmark. A chalk line on the asphalt. *Start.* His lips were soft and warm and I remember he tasted like cigarettes and honey. I never knew it was a combination I loved, but soon after I took up smoking, because Tobias did. It was something we'd do together—huddle on the fire escape of my fifth-floor walk-up, our hands chapped and shaking. It was winter by then. He was practically living with me. And we were in love.

8:38 P.M.

TOBIAS, WHAT DO YOU DO?" Conrad asks. He's ordered another bottle of Merlot and is filling a glass for Audrey, despite her mock protestations. Jessica is glancing at her watch and looking around for our server.

"I'm a photographer," he says.

Next to me, Jessica shifts in her chair.

"A man of the arts," Audrey says. "How lovely."

"You worked with some of the greats," Tobias tells her.

Audrey smiles. For the first time all night I find myself inexplicably and uncontrollably drawn to her. The way her lips part, just slightly, like she's about to spill an age-old secret.

"Bob Willoughby was my favorite," she says. "He worked for Paramount. We had quite a relationship. He had such a way with light. He used to shoot me in the very early mornings. Can you imagine? It was always dawn."

Tobias sits back. He looks satisfied. I think he told me this once about Willoughby. Sometimes Tobias would drag me out of bed in the very early mornings, too. He was always chasing the light.

"What about William Holden, really," Conrad asks. "I always wanted to know."

Audrey blushes at the mention of her rumored lover. She holds out her wineglass. Conrad chuckles. "Complicated," she says.

"That's it?" Conrad asks.

"No," she says. "But a lady never tells."

"Well, sometimes after two glasses a lady does," Conrad says.

Audrey pretends to be insulted, but I can tell she isn't, not really. She's warming to him. I can tell she likes him, and that makes me feel good—that she has someone here who can make her comfortable, make her laugh.

Audrey coughs a bit.

"What do you remember most?" Robert asks her.

She takes a small sip. She's thoughtful. It's a look that works well on her. "The early years with the children," she says. "That was all I ever wanted, really. To be a mother." She stops then, holding up her pointer finger. "Well, wait, are you asking me what I remember most, or what I enjoyed the most?"

Robert looks baffled. I realize, to him, they are, of course, the same.

"Either," he says.

"Both!" Conrad says.

"I loved *Tiffany's*," she says. "Most people think I didn't; I never really knew why." She's opening up here. She's like a drop of dye in water that begins to change the liquid. Slowly, fluidly, she becomes colored. "It was a hard shoot. I had a lot of trouble being that outgoing because I'm quite an introvert . . ." She trails off before picking back up. "But it's maybe my proudest picture. Capote and all."

"You don't say," Robert says.

"*Roman Holiday* is my favorite," Jessica says. "Sabby and I used to watch it all the time."

"It's true," I say. I remember us curled up on the couch. Burnt popcorn between us. It seems like so long ago now.

"That's very flattering," she says. "That was my first film. I remember the project fondly. Thank you."

And then, as if remembering herself, she waves her hand. "I've been going on," she says.

Conrad shakes his head. "Nonsense," he says. "We want to know." He looks straight at me.

"It's fascinating," I say. "We're all very big fans."

Tobias nods. It's true, of course. He is one. But who isn't a fan of Audrey Hepburn?

"And I would just like to say we have yet to talk about your global service," Conrad says, tapping the notebook. "Quite the humanitarian."

"No, no, it's just what we must do. Especially now."

"Especially," Conrad echoes.

"The world has become a dark place in recent years," Robert says.

Conrad shakes his head. "It always was. People are just paying attention."

"You cannot have good without evil," Audrey says. "They are like DNA strands. Intricately and irrevocably spun together. Sometimes good wins, sometimes evil does. We do not fight for good's permanent triumph, but for the balance. And so it goes."

"And so it goes," Conrad echoes.

FIVE

WE HAD THIS GAME WE USED to play, Tobias and me. Five words to describe your life right now, right this minute.

He'd ask me the question anywhere. In the shower, first thing in the morning. Sometimes over text or e-mail. On a rainy Sunday afternoon at his apartment, in an attempt to get me to confess whether I wanted pizza or Chinese. Once right in the middle of a fight.

"Five?"

The first time we played was at the end of our first date. After the Brooklyn Bridge and the movie and two bottles of cheap Spanish red, he walked me home. It felt, at that point, like we had crossed every borough line. We had been traveling forever.

He leaned in. We had been sneaking kisses all night. At the theater, when he put his arm around the back of my chair and cupped my shoulder with his palm. On the walk home. In the street, under the lights of Eighth Avenue.

"Tell me five," he said.

"Five what?"

"Five words," he said. "About what your life is like right now."

"Right *now*, right now?"

He touched the pad of my nose with his pointer. "Right. Now."

"What if I only need one?" I asked.

He leaned against the seam of my building door. Some chipped paint unhinged and dusted his jacket. Wool. Frayed at the cuffs.

"Okay," he said. "What's your one?"

"Happy."

We looked at each other. And then he pulled me into the corner with him. He put a hand on either side of my face and he kissed me. I remember feeling grounded, somehow. Like his kiss wasn't lifting me up but rooting me down. His kiss made me feel like finally, finally, I was in the spot where I belonged.

"Tell me your five," I said against his lips.

"Warm," he said, his breath on my cheek. "Open," he said, kissing my eyelid.

I breathed out against him. I grabbed the sides of his jacket and pulled.

"Fall," I said.

"Yeah. Fall's good."

"Start," he said. The way my heart felt, when he said it, it was ridiculous. I was a cartoon.

"And the last one?" I asked.

He spun me around. He pressed me against the wood. I felt my spine straighten and contract as his hands moved inside my jacket.

"Now," he said.

We made out in that doorway for a long time. It was light by the time I stumbled inside and up the stairs. When I got there Jessica was upside down on her yoga mat.

"Where have you been?" she asked me.

"Tobias," I said.

She flipped right side up. "Wow," she said. "It's seven A.M."

"We saw a movie. We walked all around the city."

"You're kidding," she said. "That's beyond romantic. I can't believe it. I can't believe it's him." She wasn't looking at me anymore. Her gaze was fixed on a spot on the ceiling. "How was it?" she asked, her eyes snapping back down to meet mine.

I sat down next to her. I didn't say a word.

"That good, huh?" She blew some air out of her lips.

"And then some. I think I'm falling in love with him." That was a lie, of course. I already had. "I bought his photo," I continued. "When I went to the photography club? They had an exhibit. He wasn't there, but I bought the photo. I never told you."

Jessica eyed me. She shook her head. "All this time," she said. "He was just out there."

"Yeah."

"Isn't that crazy? Don't you wonder why it took so long for you to find him?"

I didn't. I was just glad I had.

Those four years in between Santa Monica and the subway had been filled with reckless decisions on my part. I had moved to New York City in part for Anthony, that college boyfriend whom I didn't, despite my prior sentiments, end things with. He moved to the city after graduation, and I followed a year later. He ended things for good no sooner than my plane landed. To be fair, we had stumbled through long distance less than gracefully. I cheated. I'm sure he did, too. He was new to New York, working hundred-hour weeks and getting a banker's paycheck. He was screwing young models and expensing bottles to Goldman. I was about to start assisting at *Skyline Magazine*, a job I'd keep for approximately three months before moving over to the designer. The magazine job wasn't even a real gig—the pay was abysmal and left me babysitting nights and weekends.

Anthony and I met at Washington Square Park four days after I arrived. He told me it was over. Actually, that's not what he said. What he said was: "I'm not ready." I cried for weeks even though I didn't care, even though I knew it didn't mean anything. I listened to bad R&B music. I lost five pounds. But it wasn't really heartbreak. I wouldn't know that until Tobias. It was just disappointment. I was going through the motions. Jessica sat on the floor with me and baked pot brownies and we watched *Casablanca* for reasons I can no longer remember. *We'll always have Paris?* There were a string of affairs after that, all of them some shade of wrong. Jessica comforted and quelled. She held on to love like a floatie in a shark-infested ocean. And sometimes I resented her for that—her unfettered belief that it was all going to work out—but not today. Today I loved it.

Jessica twisted her legs underneath her. "This feels like the start, doesn't it?" she said. "Right now. What if he's the one?"

For Jessica, everything had always been about some kind of trajectory. Marriage. Kids. A house. Jessica was still with Sumir, and they'd been through every stage of adulthood together—virginity, graduation, first jobs.

But in those early years of Tobias and me, it was never about the way we were going to end up. It was only ever about where we were in the moment.

A sign on our wall mocked me. WHAT YOU PLANT NOW, YOU WILL HARVEST LATER.

Jessica lifted herself up from the floor and went into the kitchen. "Love is in the air!" she called over her shoulder. It was.

8:54 P.M.

I NEED TO PUMP," JESSICA WHISPERS to me.

She's holding her blazer out from her swollen breasts.

"Do you have your thing?" I ask. Despite seeing her walking around with that contraption strapped to her chest that milks her like a cow—*swoosh swoosh swoosh*—I don't really have any idea how it works. Or how big it is.

"I'll just duck into the bathroom," she says. "I brought it with me."

"Can you do that?" Tobias asks.

It takes me a moment to realize that he's talking to us, that he heard and then that he's referring to Jessica getting up and leaving. If she stands and removes herself from the table, will she be able to come back?

"I'm leaking," she says. "I guess we'll find out."

She pushes back her chair and slings her bag over her shoulder.

We all watch her, but nothing happens. She disappears around the corner, and then Conrad calls our attention back.

"I think our theme is getting stale," Conrad says. "Let's play a game while we wait for dinner to arrive."

Tobias puts his elbows on the table. "But we were just getting to the good stuff," he says. "Love was on deck."

"Better to feel our way into that one," Conrad says. "We've been talking about it yet, and we will talk about it still."

"Fair enough."

Audrey purses her lips. She puts her hand on Conrad's forearm and he immediately falls quiet. "What happened with you two?" she asks. She's talking to Tobias and me.

Tobias looks at me. It's the first time since we sat down that I allow my gaze to meet his.

"I guess we wanted different things," he says.

I swivel my eyes to the table. I forbid them from rolling. He picks up on my annoyance immediately. I'm not being coy. "Is that not true?" he asks me.

"We wanted different things? You're serious."

Tobias crosses his arms against his chest. "I don't know."

"We both wanted everything," I say. "That was the problem."

"I never had a problem with that."

"Yes, you did. Do you remember that day in Great Barrington? You told me you were sure we weren't supposed to have to fight so hard for something."

"Yeah," he said. "I stand by that."

"So how were you okay with it?"

"With what? Us being together?"

I nod.

"Because," he says. "I was. I just wasn't okay with how miserable you were."

Audrey waves her hand. "I'm sorry," she says. "This is a unique situation. Perhaps we're getting to the heart too quickly."

Tobias shakes his head. "It's all the same now. It's all the past."

The past. I want to say something else, but I stop. Because I'm not sure if I want that piece on the table yet. It's a familiar feeling, this one of hesitation. There were times when dating Tobias felt like playing Jenga. How much can I say? If I reveal this, will the whole tower collapse? If I tell him how I really feel, will that be my last turn? It was terrifying and exhilarating because every time I took another piece out and the tower stood, I felt like I'd won. What I didn't remember is that at some point in a game, the entire tower falls. It happens every single time. It is the only way the game ends. Why then did I keep playing, knowing that I would be left with rubble?

SIX

THE DAY AFTER OUR FIRST DATE he showed up at my apartment. It was three P.M. on a Saturday. Jessica wasn't home; she was spending the day driving around upstate with Sumir, looking at country houses they couldn't afford.

I was painting my toenails in the window. It was a summer encore in fall, and I had on ankle jeans and a tank top. He rang the buzzer; I didn't hear it. Then he called my name. My bedroom looked out onto Tenth Avenue and I saw him, five floors below, squinting up into the sun.

"Hey," I yelled.

He waved.

"Do you want to come up?"

He shook his head. "I want you to come down."

"I'm painting my toes," I said. I shook the bottle out the window. It was neon blue. *Night Racer.*

"I'll wait," he said. He gestured across the street. "Coffee." I saw him walk into the Empire Diner and take a seat at a window table. I shuffled my still-wet toes through the straps of flip-flops and raced down the stairs. My heart hum-hum-hummmmmed in my chest as I crossed the street to join him.

"Oh good," he said when I came in. He got up from the booth, set a five-dollar bill on the table, took my hand, and walked outside.

"I thought you wanted coffee?"

"No way we're spending today inside," he said.

He spun me into him. There were times when being with him felt like dancing. The waltz, the two-step, sometimes the jitterbug, always the tango.

"What are you doing here?" I asked, now a bit breathless.

"I was thinking about you. And I thought that was stupid."

"Stupid?" I stiffened in his arms.

"Yep, stupid. Why sit around and think about you when I could see you?"

He kissed me. We started walking. I didn't care where we were going, but I asked anyway.

"The water," he said. "If you want to?" He was sometimes shy like this. A little unsure. It came at the strangest intervals.

We swung hands. We ran across intersections. We veered off after Fourteenth Street and crossed over to the Hudson.

It was almost four by the time we got there. I hadn't bothered to bring a sweater. We plopped down on the grassy lawn of one of the piers and Tobias took off his sweatshirt. He draped it over my shoulders and I threaded my arms through. It smelled like him. Like cigarettes and honey and a faint ocean breeze. "Thanks," I said.

I'd keep that sweatshirt even after he left, because it still smelled like him. I didn't wash it, but I slept in it, and after a while it reeked of sweat and my coconut shampoo and I had to admit it was just a sweatshirt. He was gone.

He lay down on his back. I did the same. We didn't touch, but I could feel his body next to mine. It felt like we were both sinking down into the earth, becoming a part of it. Like we'd meet there— somewhere at the center among raw, fresh dirt. Where things begin.

"I love New York," I said. It felt like a really generic thing to say, but it was actually how I felt.

"I think I could live in Portland," he said. "I have that dream. Wake up and go hiking. Cook. Listen to the rain."

"Wear a lot of Patagonia."

"Yeah." He laced his fingers through mine. "But somewhere with real quality of life. Somewhere quiet. I love Brooklyn, but sometimes I wonder if this is the best version of my life."

"Of course not," I say. "The best version is hanging out on some yacht in Monaco, photographing Victoria's Secret models."

"Commercial photography isn't really my thing."

"I pray that's sarcasm," I said. I didn't bother to turn my head to check, though.

"Fifty-fifty."

That was something Tobias said. *Fifty-fifty.* In the beginning, I loved it. It proved he was complicated, that he refused a bottom line. I thought it meant he saw truth in things that were frivolous, and frivolity in things that were fundamental. It was a way of looking at the world that allowed the air in. But after a few years it just began to confuse me. It was like shifting sands—I couldn't tell anymore what was real to him. When I'd ask if he was mad at me, and he said "fifty-fifty," what did that mean?

I shivered in his sweatshirt. The wind blew. In front of us Jersey City grew out from the water.

"I have a popcorn maker and *Roman Holiday* on DVD," he said next to me. "Let's blow this Popsicle stand."

He was compelling and sexy and the universe was working us together *and* he liked Audrey Hepburn. I felt like I had sidestepped into a different reality—the kind that houses young royals and celebrities. People who were always smiling, because what was there to be concerned about? Life was glorious.

We went back to his apartment. A loft on Woodpoint with bright blue walls and huge, half-painted canvases hanging from them.

"My roommate is an artist," Tobias said. "Well, one of them." There were five bedrooms all in a row, but only Tobias and Matty were ever home. Two of the roommates were archaeologists on a dig in Egypt. I only ever met them once, on the day Tobias moved out of the loft. One had a serious girlfriend who lived in Greenpoint (the artist), and the other was Matty, a quiet, nineteen-year-old computer science major at Brooklyn College. Matty's family had emigrated from the Dominican Republic when he was three months old, and although he looked sixteen sometimes, there was a maturity to him that was always there. Tobias called Matty his best friend, which I came to realize was true. They were an unlikely pair. Tobias was impatient and spontaneous—all curls and gold and air. Matty was methodical and predictable and happy to play the sidekick. Even in college, he was already paying half his parents' rent in the Bronx.

"Matty boy!" he said when we walked in. "I got a girl."

I nudged him in the ribs.

Matty poked his head out of the third room. There was a sign on the door that read STUDY SESSION IN PROGRESS with a photo of a girl sitting on a desk, her legs around a guy in a chair. I immediately knew Tobias had bought it for him.

"Hello," he said to me. He extended his hand, but he didn't come out from behind the door.

I took it. "Hi."

"We're gonna toss on a little Audrey Hepburn. Wanna join?"

Matty poked his head out farther.

"He's part groundhog," Tobias said. "Don't take it personally."

"I love groundhogs," I said.

Tobias grinned at me. He slung his arm over my shoulder and squeezed. "So do I, Sabrina. So do I."

"I have an econ exam tomorrow," Matty said. "But if you watch at normal volume I'll be able to hear."

"Multitasking," Tobias said. "I love it."

Matty closed his door.

"Funny," I mouthed.

"Sweet," he mouthed back.

Matty was nineteen to our twenty-three, and at the time those four years felt like decades—expanses of time that allowed us to be older, wiser, weathered. Sometimes, we felt like his parents, although we weren't entitled to. Matty was smarter than both of us.

"Come here," Tobias said.

He pulled me on top of him. We started making out. His hands found my hips and then the small of my back. He threaded them up under my tank top. I sighed out into his mouth.

"Let's can the movie," I whispered.

"We can multitask, too," he said. He drew me in for a deep kiss and then got up from the couch and popped the movie in. I watched his back—I was still wearing his sweatshirt, and he just had a thin gray T-shirt. It stretched and bent as he moved, like a dancer warming up.

He pulled down a projector screen from the ceiling just as the opening music swelled somewhere in the apartment.

"Movie viewing, deconstructed," I said.

He turned around and gave me a funny look.

"What? It's cool," I said quickly, and he rolled his eyes.

"You win," he said.

The movie was playing, but I never got to see it. Because he picked up my hand and led me down the corridor to the fifth bedroom. A small room with a double bed, blue sheets, and bookshelves. They covered every wall. Cheerful clutter.

He put his hands on my face. He bent me backward, and my head landed on the bed. There wasn't anywhere else to go.

"Well, look at that," I said.

"Yeah," he said, "look at that."

9:02 P.M.

J ESSICA SCURRIES BACK TO THE TABLE, stuffing the pump into her bag. "Sorry, sorry," she says. "But I'm back!"

Our starters have been cleared (I didn't get any crudo), but what Audrey says is: "I believe we began to turn the corner on this." She gestures across the table at Tobias and me.

Jessica tosses her bag down and runs her hands through her hair. "Sabby and Tobias?"

Conrad leans forward. He points at Jessica. "You," he says, "might be the only true teller of this tale."

"Oh no," Tobias says. "We're in trouble then."

Jessica gives him a look of mock anger, and my heart squeezes remembering how they used to be with each other—how the three of us were.

Audrey looks confused. Conrad chuckles. Robert pushes back his chair. "Why is that?"

"No," Jessica says, taking a sip of wine. Since the baby, she's started drinking again. She glances at me. "Do you really want me to say?"

I extend my hand. "Whatever," I say. "This conversation is already pretty deep in there."

"It was ten years," Jessica says cautiously. She keeps her eyes on Tobias. "It was a very long road. I—" She exhales. "Are you sure?"

"Please," Conrad says. "Go on."

"They loved each other. Sometimes I think that was the problem. It was too much; it made things hard when they shouldn't have been."

"Sometimes love isn't easy," Audrey says.

"If you're with the wrong person," Jessica says. She catches herself and her eyes go wide. She just corrected Audrey Hepburn.

"I think she's right," Robert says.

"Ringing endorsement." I can't help myself.

"You didn't think they were right for one another?" Audrey asks.

"I did," Jessica says. "At first. For a long time, really. But . . . they kept not growing up. Sometimes I felt like their relationship kept them perpetually the age they were when they met."

"You were eighteen when you met Sumir," I say. "That's not fair."

"You never got anywhere," Jessica says.

"Why does there always have to be a destination?" I ask. "Aren't you the one who was always talking about the journey? You used to believe in things like that—in the flow of life, or whatever."

"*Life* is forward moving," Jessica says. "I'm not saying you had to get married. I'm just saying you needed to be evolving, and you weren't."

I pinch the bridge of my nose with my thumb and forefinger. Tobias turns toward us. "In some ways you're right," he says to her.

"Duh." She smiles at him.

"I loved her," he says. His eyes find mine. "My whole life—it's always been her."

Before I have a chance to let his words settle, Jessica cuts in. "I know that," she says. "I never doubted that part."

I think about the two years we spent apart. When he went to California and worked as a photographer's assistant for some rock-and-roll guy in Santa Monica.

"What does it matter?" I say. "Tobias said it himself: it's in the past."

"Because isn't that why we're here?" Audrey says.

I look around the table. "I thought there was something essential about us," I say. "That we were fundamental. That we were just destined to fit back together."

Jessica exhales loudly. "But I'm not sure you fit at *all*. Tobias has always been a flower."

Jessica has this theory that people in relationships are either flowers or gardeners. Two flowers shouldn't partner; they need someone to support them, to help them grow.

"I liked him that way."

"And you?" Audrey asks.

"I'm a gardener," I say. "That wasn't our problem. That worked."

Jessica shakes her head. She picks up her wine. She seems, all at once, unabashedly sad. "You weren't a gardener," she says. "This turned you into one."

SEVEN

I THINK YOU'RE AN ORCHID."

That's what Tobias said to me as we lay in his tiny, narrow bed in his five-bedroom apartment listening to the end notes of *Roman Holiday* playing somewhere outside. It sounded dreamy, far-off. Matty had come out of his den to make food, and I heard him in the open kitchen, dancing around with the microwave.

"You think I'm a flower?"

Tobias propped himself up on his elbow. He traced the terrain of my shoulder with his fingertips. Up the curve, down through the crevice of my collarbone.

"Of course."

"We're in trouble, then," I said. I had just told him about Jessica's theory. I don't know why. Sex does that sometimes. It smooths time out. It makes you think it's okay to be farther down the road, somewhere you're not yet ready to be.

"We are?" He put his lips where his fingers were. I threaded my hands through his hair. "Doesn't feel like it."

"Well, you're clearly a flower."

"I am?"

"You are. And two flowers can't be together."

I remember holding my breath then. *Be together*. Did I use the phrase too soon? What did I even mean by it? I knew what I meant. Already, I meant everything. I meant live, work, create, breathe. I meant entwine our lives until they could not be separated—but that's insane to think after knowing someone for barely seventy-two hours.

The problem, of course, was that I believed I had known him since that day in Santa Monica. I had known him for four years.

"How come?" was all he said.

"There are flowers and there are gardeners. Flowers bloom; gardeners tend. Two flowers, no tending. Everything dies."

"Or becomes overrun," he said. He kissed me some more. It helped. "Who came up with this again?"

"My roommate."

"Your roommate." He pulled back. He squinted at me. "No offense," he said. "But that seems pretty boiled down and not altogether accurate."

"None taken. It's not my theory."

"But you believe it?"

I let my head fall back against the pillow. "Yeah," I said. "I do. I think there are two roles in a relationship." Again, why did I use that word? *Relationship*. It sounded so clunky right there, stuck in the middle of our conversation. "The person who's the base and the person who's the height."

"I'd never want to stop anyone from growing," he said.

"But you're not a gardener."

"Why can't we grow together?" He looked at me, and I knew he didn't mean in general, as a rule. I knew he meant us.

"Maybe we can," I said.

We had sex again, but this time was different. The first time was fun and awkward and somewhat apologetic—as first-time sex often is, when more is on the line. But this time it was like we were really taking it to heart. The whole idea of it. Two people becoming one.

Later Matty joined us for dinner—this hole-in-the-wall Indian place on Bedford that had the best daal and tamarind chutney. We'd go there often in the years after. Sometimes me and Matty, sometimes me and Tobias, sometimes Matty and Tobias. That night, we held hands under the table. We talked about going to India and giggled because we both knew what the other was thinking—what we wanted to say—*let's go together*. But despite our intimate afternoon it was still too new. I didn't want to break the spell with even a promise of what was to come. It was too delicate—all air, clouds, the mirrored haze of a giant bubble. It had yet to solidify.

"How was the movie?" Matty asked.

"Illuminating," Tobias said, running his thumb over my wrist.

"Great," I said.

Tobias raised his eyebrows at me. Matty tore off a piece of naan. "I don't think it's her best work," he said. Matty was serious about things that didn't require his attention sometimes—restaurant reviews, movies that had been put to bed decades ago.

"No?" Tobias leaned forward on the table. It shook from the weight transference.

"*Breakfast at Tiffany's*," Matty said, "that's the classic."

"You know just because something is well known doesn't mean it's great or even good," Tobias said.

"Of course not," Matty countered. "But most of the time it's popular for a reason. Popularity means people like it, and isn't there a strong correlation between pleasure and quality?"

"Is that true?" I asked. "I think it might just be name recognition. I mean, do the majority of people like *Breakfast at Tiffany's*, or do the majority of people just *know* about *Breakfast at Tiffany's*? She's in every college girl's dorm room. Well, her and Eiffel Tower figurines."

"It's the same thing," Matty said. "The majority of people know about it *because* it's her best film."

"That's like saying the Nazis were good because people knew about them," I said.

"I didn't say good," Matty said. "I said great. As in well known, making their mark on history, et cetera."

Tobias moved his hand to cup the back of my neck. "Let it go," he said. "Matty doesn't know how not to win."

"It's not winning," Matty said. "It's just a question of obvious truth."

Tobias laughed, and so did I. Matty had that effect on us—he could bring us together simply by being himself. Whether it was an alignment of opinion on Matty (what he was wearing, how he'd talk to a girl), or his beliefs—it didn't matter. When the three of us were together, Tobias and I were always on the same side.

"Where did you meet her?" Matty asked, cocking his head in my direction.

"Stuck underground," Tobias said at the same time I said: "At the beach."

Tobias looked amused. "At the beach?"

I hadn't yet told him about our first meeting. I liked that I had this secret about us. It was like a card I had tucked away. One I could hold and play when I really needed it. I didn't know why I just tossed it down then.

But something about Tobias was always forcing me to be honest, be open, fess up. Honesty first. Honesty always. That was his motto.

When Jessica and I were twenty-three, we went and saw His Holiness the Dalai Lama speak in Times Square. Jessica arranged it. She had seen a flyer in the halls of NYU and entered some lottery by which we got not just to go, but also to have actual seats. We were still probably two thousand people away from him, but the energy he put out was palpable. Jessica cried. I couldn't really speak.

Here is what I remember him saying: *Kindness before honesty.*

We are taught that honesty is the most important quality. Tell the truth. Do not lie. Etc. But there are so many instances when honesty isn't kind. When the kinder thing to do is to keep what you have to say to yourself.

Tobias didn't understand that. He told me everything. Eventually, so did I. But as the honesty grew, so did the cruelty. Sometimes I thought we were being honest just to see how deep we could cut.

"*Ashes and Snow*," I said. "We talked by the photo of the boy with eagle wings."

Under the table, Tobias dropped my hand. "I don't understand."

"I knew you when I saw you underground," I said. "I mean, I recognized you." I ran a hand through my hair. I could feel my cheeks heating up. "I sound crazy."

Matty looked back and forth between us like he was watching a sporting event in its last fifteen seconds.

Tobias sat back in his chair. He ran a hand over his forehead. "*Ashes and Snow*? That was, what, four years ago?"

"Yeah," I said. "I was in college. I went with a class. It's not a big deal."

"Yes," he said. "It is."

I almost asked him if he was mad, but I didn't.

"I don't remember," he said finally.

I cared, more than I let on. He should have remembered. I could never have forgotten.

"I wasn't sure," I said. It was a lie, but it felt like a good compromise.

"But then you were."

"I guess. It's a funny coincidence, that's all."

"Coincidence," Matty repeated. "Ridiculous notion."

We both stared at him.

"All events in the universe are occurring at random," he said. "There is no such thing as order. Chaos is king."

"Then why do you insist on hospital corners?" Tobias asked.

I breathed out a sigh of relief.

"Because," Matty said. "I can't think in the mess."

"Walking contradiction," Tobias said. To me: "Did you like it?"

"The exhibit?"

He smiled. "Yes."

"I loved it."

Tobias nodded. "I don't think I liked it."

"You're kidding." I mixed some green pea rice and curry on my plate. "You said all these things about that photograph."

"I did?"

"Space and nature, and . . . I don't know. You liked it back then. You said you'd been a few times."

Matty chewed thoughtfully. "He used to have pretty shitty taste in art. Still sometimes does."

Under the table Tobias kicked Matty. "Dude, come on."

"I'm serious," Matty said. "You had a Thomas Kinkade poster framed." Matty pointed his fork. "I could not make that crap up if I tried."

"It was the nineties when I came of age," Tobias said. "I liked Disney."

"Fucking depressing," Matty muttered through a bite.

"Who is Thomas Kinkade?" I asked.

"You know those bucolic paintings of cottages? That eventually had Disney characters wandering through?"

"Kinda." I didn't. But I liked hearing him talk about it. It felt like this incredibly vulnerable opening in him—like a patch of his body where the skin hadn't fully fused.

"My mom used to have them hanging in her bedroom. I don't know. They reminded me of my childhood." He looked at Matty. "You done?"

"Not even close," Matty said. "But she can figure some things out for herself."

"Some girls might find my sensitive nature charming," Tobias said, extending an arm over the back of my chair.

"Not her," Matty said. "She's smart, I can tell."

Tobias grinned at me. "Well, that we can agree on."

9:10 P.M.

THE RESTAURANT IS BUSY. WAITERS WEAVE in and out of tables. The tinkling sound of champagne glasses reaches us from another table. People are celebrating.

They bring out dinner. A plate of steaming saffron risotto shaped into a perfect mound, delicate Parmesan-and-sage tagliatelle in a butter-cream sauce, and steak with a sprig of rosemary. Everything is so neat and orderly and for a moment I regret that we are not at some casual Italian bistro, some corner joint where we share everything, wine spills on the table, and everyone shouts over one another. There is something so familiar about those meals. Jovial. Maybe that would have lightened the mood. But then I remember Jessica asked me where I wanted to go on my birthday and I chose here. It's been our tradition since we met—we take each other out on our birthdays. So many things have slipped through the cracks over the past few years, but this one has stuck around. All at once, I feel grateful for that. For whatever alchemy led us here.

"This looks delicious," Robert says. "You know I came here once with . . . on business." He clears his throat. "I remember it being good."

"Heartily agree. The wife and I used to frequent it often," Conrad says.

"Were the tablecloths red?" Audrey asks. "I remember them being red."

"You've all been here?" I ask, stunned.

"Of course," Audrey says. "It would have had to be somewhere we could find." She winks at me. I feel the way I did when I first walked in: bowled over by what is happening here.

Conrad picks up his wineglass. "A toast!" he hollers.

"To what?" Audrey asks. She grabs at her collar. It is a little warm in here, or maybe the wine is finally settling. We're drinking a deep Barolo now. Conrad has stealthily ordered another bottle.

"To sharing a meal together," Conrad says. He shrugs, like it seems as good a toast as any.

"And making new friends," Audrey adds.

"Thank you all for coming," I say, because I cannot think of anything else.

"To Sabrina," Robert says. He's holding up his water glass with a mixture of pride and hesitation.

"Happy Birthday," Tobias says.

"Yes!" Conrad says. "Happy Birthday."

We clink glasses. Next to me, Jessica yawns. "I feel like we were just getting somewhere interesting," she says.

"This has all been pretty interesting," Tobias says. I can't tell if it's sarcasm; his tone is right on the edge. Fifty-fifty.

"I feel a lot of regret," Robert says. The table falls silent. Jessica and Conrad begin to pick at their plates.

"There is a lot of loss here," Audrey says. She reaches an arm across the table and squeezes Robert's hand. "I can feel my own, in a way, as well."

"Thank you," he says. His voice sounds heavy. He clears his throat.

"Sometimes I think that the only true way we can ever know a thing's value is by losing it." This from Conrad.

Audrey looks at him. There is tenderness in her eyes. She's become maternal in the last few minutes.

"So how can we ever be happy?" Tobias asks.

"Happiness is not constantly needing things to be at their full potential," Jessica says.

"That's depressing," I say.

"That's *true*," Jessica says. She looks up from her plate. "Like I don't get happiness from having a perfect day with Sumir. I get happiness from accepting that I rarely, if ever, have a perfect day with Sumir. My happiness is accepting that ninety-five percent of the time my life is deeply imperfect."

Conrad winks at her. "Well done," he says. He takes a forkful of scallop and pops it into his mouth. "Delightful," he murmurs.

I wag a finger back and forth between them. "You two are the most positive people I know. In college you gave me a C because I, and I quote, 'neglected to see the simple beauty and overcomplicated everything.'"

"Wasn't so positive for you," Conrad mutters, chuckling.

"You're missing the point," Robert says. He's cutting his steak, and he puts his knife down.

I stiffen. He notices.

"The simple beauty, as you put it, is from things not always aligning. There is no simple beauty in perfection."

"I disagree," Tobias says. "To me the simplest beauty is nature. And nature is nothing if not perfect."

Next to me, Jessica balks. "Oh, come on," she says. "That's so generic."

"Is it? I think actually it's pretty profound."

"No," she says. "It's not profound. It's easy to sit there and spout poetry about nature and its beauty, or whatever, but it's immature. You guys have no idea what goes into having an actually simple life."

"Enlighten us," Tobias says. He sits back and crosses his forearms over his abdomen. His food remains untouched.

I feel, sitting here, physically pulled between them. Jessica loved Tobias, but she didn't love the relationship we had. I thought it was because she didn't understand it. It was so much less linear than anything in her own life.

Jessica straightens up. "An actually simple life means putting your husband's shoes away when he leaves them by the door even though you've reminded him one thousand times. And not saying anything about it."

"That just sounds like compromising," I say.

"Not compromising," Audrey says. "Compromise."

We all turn to look at her. She gives us one of her dazzling movie-star smiles. "I was married, you know," she says.

"What happened?" Those of us who love Audrey know the stories of her two marriages. Abuse, maybe? Jealousy. Regret. Her painful road to motherhood. Three miscarriages, a fall from a horse that left her in permanent pain. For someone with a perfect public image, Audrey had a tragic personal life.

"I had to dim my light," she says grimly. "It was not an easy thing to be married to a celebrity. But it's also not an easy thing to be married to darkness. Eventually I dimmed so far I extinguished."

At this, Conrad laughs. It's an odd reaction to her heartfelt sentiment. "You do have a way with words," he says, half to himself.

To my surprise, Audrey smiles. "Why, thank you. I always liked writing. I did a little of it from time to time."

"I'd like to return to this idea of compromise," Robert says. He has his hand in the air, like we're in a classroom.

"By all means," Conrad says.

"How do you know at any given moment what is giving enough, and what is giving too much? As Audrey would attest, marriage for the sake of marriage is no prize at all." Audrey nods. Jessica shifts.

"I think it takes work," Audrey says. She takes a small bite of her food, chews, and swallows.

"How much?" Robert.

"I don't know," Audrey says. "I always gave too much or little—they were equally damning."

"A lot," Jessica says, a little frustrated. "It takes a lot of work."

"You mentioned your wife," Tobias says to Conrad. "You got married?"

"Naturally," Conrad says.

"How long?"

Conrad sets down his fork. "Thirty-five years."

"And?"

Conrad pauses for a moment. A move I recognize. He was always doing this in class: taking an opportunity for dramatic effect. "We never wanted to get divorced at the same time."

"That's brilliant," Jessica says. She fumbles around in her purse and pulls out a half-bent Moleskine. "Shit," she says, still looking.

Conrad unhooks the pen from his outside pocket and holds it across the table. Tobias passes it to her over me.

She writes it down hastily, tearing off the page and stuffing it into her pocket.

"What happened to the girl who used to write *love is the answer* on our bathroom mirror?" I ask her.

"Love is still the answer," she says.

"It's the questions that stop mattering so much," Audrey says.

Will we work out? Can we sustain this? How could I possibly be with anyone else?

Those were the questions I used to ask myself all the time. I asked them constantly. I asked them at the door to this restaurant and I am asking them now, with him sitting beside me still.

EIGHT

"TOBIAS, THIS IS JESSICA. JESSICA, TOBIAS."

"The famous man," Jessica said.

Tobias cocked his head at her. "I hope that's a good thing."

"The best." Jessica was sitting on the dirty white couch in our living room, her legs curled up under her and an oversized shawl over her shoulders. She'd bought it in New Mexico on a meditation retreat she'd gone on the summer before. I wanted to go but didn't have the cash. For a week of camping and silence, five hundred dollars seemed like a lot of money. She'd sold her bedroom air-conditioning unit to help pay for it. The following summer she spent nearly entirely at Sumir's.

"Well, that's a relief," Tobias said. He looked from Jessica to me and back. "Sabrina is pretty famous in my world, too."

My stomach flipped.

"I feel like I already know you," Jessica said. "I've been the captain of your search party."

Tobias smiled, although if he was amused or confused I couldn't necessarily say. I shot Jessica a cool-it look. He didn't know about the UCLA endeavor.

"I like it here," he said instead. He started looking around. I peered at our apartment through his eyes. The hanging stained-glass pendant in the window, the pile of Moroccan meditation cushions, the mismatched curtains—like stepping into a crystal shop, without the incense. We had a lot of stuff.

"We like it, too," I said.

Tobias shifted onto his left foot beside me. We had left his apartment because we wanted time to be alone together, and Matty was in a talkative mood, which meant shutting the door was impossible. Sex with Tobias was something I could not get enough of. With old boyfriends it had felt like this separate thing—something different in tone and resonance from the rest of our relationship. Time out of time. But with Tobias it was an extension. He made love the way he lived—close, intense, on the edge. Maybe that's why it was impactful. Every time we were in bed I had the sense, even underlying, that it might be the last.

Right then I just wanted to lock him in my bedroom. Usually on the weekends Jessica was at Sumir's. It hadn't occurred to me she would be home.

"What are you guys up to?" Jessica asked.

"Just hanging out," I said. "Where's Sumir?"

Jessica looked around like she was surprised he wasn't there. "He had to work," she said. "Hey, do you guys want to get brunch?"

Tobias didn't say anything. "We ate," I answered.

Jessica hopped off the couch, tucking her shawl around her. "Is it cold out?"

I couldn't answer. I had no idea what the temperature was. We had spent the entire subway ride like two teenagers who had no place to go. Cold? For us it was July in November.

"A little," Tobias said. "Jacket, no hat."

Jessica beamed at him. "Thanks." To me: "He's taller than I thought he'd be."

I rolled my eyes and laughed; so did Tobias.

She went into her bedroom. "Nice to meet you!" she called over her shoulder.

Tobias's hands found my hips. He pushed me back against the living room wall. "Not here," I breathed.

"Show me where."

I led him into my bedroom. The windows were open and it was cold and loud. Tenth Avenue was a riot of noise. I shut one. I pulled the other down until there was a gap of half a foot.

I turned around to find Tobias sitting on my bed. He was looking up at the wall separating my two windows. My stomach instantly turned in on itself, because I knew what he was seeing.

"The photo," he said.

The one. A man, eyes closed, covered in a cloud of smoke. His own work. The photo I'd bought and carried with me through two campus apartments and finally here, to New York, where I had, after two years, taken it out from under my bed, had it framed, and hung it up. It read like a map, kind a symbol, like a prophecy. And Tobias knew it.

"How did you . . ." But it wasn't a question, not exactly.

I froze. I could not physically move. I didn't know if that was good, or the end. What if he was freaked out? Didn't this make me worse than a stalker?

"I think I've been looking for you, too," he said. He didn't say it to me. He said it to the photograph. I went to him then. We made love for the first time in my bed. It felt like we were making up for lost time. But afterward, and for years later, I couldn't help but think of the way he said it, what had his attention. *I've been looking for you.*

Maybe he meant the man. Maybe he meant the photo. Maybe it wasn't me after all.

9:16 P.M.

I WANT TO GET BACK TO THE NIGHT I was born," I say. This is too much talk about Tobias. I'm not ready to deal with it. I'm beginning to realize it's more complicated than I previously believed, the reason that he's here.

Robert pauses mid-bite.

"Absolutely," Audrey says. "Let's do that." She's becoming comfortable in her role of facilitator. Conrad can prod; she can foster. They're a team, and I see from the way he refills her glass and she passes him bread that they feel the shared responsibility, too.

"What do you want to know?" Robert says. He puts down his fork and dabs at the corner of his mouth with his napkin. The move strikes me as oddly formal, and I get a rush of anger at how reserved he is. Appropriate. I can't imagine this man in the blue suit with the salt-and-pepper hair throwing a chair out of the window in a rage.

But he did.

"I want to know if you were sick then," I say.

"Yes," Robert says immediately, no hesitation. "Of course." He looks confused, and across the table I see Conrad take a big inhale.

"You want to know if you're responsible," Conrad says to me. "If you made him that way."

"That's ridiculous," Jessica chimes in next to me. "How could Sabrina be responsible? Robert was an alcoholic who left his family in the lurch. She was a *child*."

Conrad doesn't say anything; neither does Audrey. Tobias is the one who speaks.

"You weren't," he says right to me. I feel him reach for my hand under the table but I move it away. Doesn't he know? Doesn't he remember he was the one who left me? That they both were?

Robert shifts in his seat. "I'll tell you anything you want to know," he says.

I look past Tobias to this man who is supposed to be my father. The physical resemblance I see. It just becomes more prominent the longer we sit here. Maybe it's the surprise factor that makes it so noticeable. My mother never mentioned it. She'd never say something like *You have your father's nose*. I'm sure she noticed, though. I'm sure it hurt.

"Where are my sisters?" I ask. *Sisters*. What a word.

Robert busies himself with his napkin again. Is he going to cry? It's hard to say. I don't know his tells.

"Alexandra is an orthodontist. Or she will be next year. Daisy is studying film. She wants to be a director and writer. She's—" But he breaks off. I know he was going to say *talented*. He should be able to gush about them; they're his children. But it makes me feel light-headed—these details, the ways in which he knows them.

"Where do they live?"

"Daisy is here, in New York. Alexandra lives in California. She has a baby."

"She's married?"

Robert shakes his head. "Yes. He works a lot. Her mother helps out with the baby."

"How lovely; she must adore her." From Audrey.

"Him," Robert says. "Oliver. Alexandra is a wonderful mother." He looks at me. "It would have been nice, for you to know her." He doesn't say the rest. He doesn't say *your mother wouldn't allow it.* He doesn't need to.

"I think she was afraid of having to share me," I say, because I feel I need to defend her. She is, after all, not here. And she was a good mother—still is. Distracted, overworked, but present in the ways that mattered. Food, shelter, care. She told me she loved me every day. By all accounts, I have been tremendously blessed. By all accounts, my life was better without him in it.

"Naturally," Audrey says.

Robert runs a hand over his forehead. "She had good reason to keep you away," he says. "I don't blame her. It's very important you know that."

I think about how little we talked about Robert, my mother and I. Would it have been different had I pressed her? Should I have? "Fine," I say.

"I don't want you to think after tonight that she's somehow the bad guy. I am the bad guy. I will always be the bad guy. There is nothing that could change that."

"Then what is the point of all this?" I ask. I throw my hands up for effect. For the first time since we sat down I want to get up and walk out the door. I seriously consider it. I also need a cigarette. I have been continuously quitting since Tobias and I broke up, but it has never quite stuck. I don't chain-smoke, but in tense situations I can never seem to hang on without sneaking out for one. I have my emergency pack in the bottom of my bag, too.

"Five," Tobias says next to me. It's quiet—he leans a little my way when he says it, but everyone else still hears.

"Frustrated," I say. I shoot it at him.

"Good," Tobias says. "And?"

"Sad." I look down at my plate. "Time."

"Yes."

Conrad and Audrey are watching us with a quiet curiosity. I don't look at Jessica; she knows the game. I'm surprised when she volunteers one.

"Memory," she says.

"Okay. Memory. You need one more."

I inhale. I remember the first time we added this word to our five. I see the scene in my mind. I know he's seeing it, too. Before I have a chance to say it.

"Love," he says. As if it's obvious. As if it's inevitable.

"Ah," Conrad says. He sits forward. His eyes flit back and forth from Tobias to Robert to Jessica to me, like he's watching passing trees out of a moving car window. "We've arrived."

NINE

T OBIAS AND I WERE HUDDLED on my fire escape, a cigarette
between us. Or I should say between his fingertips. But we were
sharing it. This was early. I hadn't yet admitted that I smoked.

We had spent the day browsing McNally Jackson, my favorite
bookstore, downtown, and walking around SoHo. We'd picked up
slices at Ben's Pizza around eleven A.M., but that was the last time
we'd eaten, and it was now close to seven.

Jessica was out with Sumir for dinner. I was starving, but I hadn't
said anything yet. I didn't want to risk fracturing the afternoon by
tracking down dinner, and I knew all we had in our fridge were
mossy pitas and mustard.

I would come to understand that food was something Tobias didn't
necessarily crave, although he was great in the kitchen. He could
cook a perfect meal, but he could also go a full day without eating,

only remembering when his body started roaring with hunger. He ate to live. Sometimes I think he was so filled up by other things that there wasn't any room.

But not me. My stomach rumbled audibly. Tobias scooted closer to me. "What was that?" He patted my abdomen. It tickled.

"Hunger," I said.

"Hunger is pretty dramatic."

"Do not start," I warned. I was teasing. It was one of our first exchanges of this nature, and the familiarity of mock annoyance filled me with a very specific kind of exhilarating joy.

Tobias put his hand on the side of my face and kissed me. "It's my duty to feed you. Let's go to dinner."

He snuffed the cigarette out and climbed back through the window, offering me his hand. The cigarette went into the trash and we followed each other toward the door.

"Where do you want to go?" I asked, searching for a lone Ugg boot that had drifted behind the little bench we kept in the foyer, if you could call it a foyer. It was a wall and a small bench with some boots underneath, and an umbrella stand.

Tobias stamped his heel into his sneaker. "There's this bistro pretty close to here I love. I'd like to take you there."

Whatever he loved, I wanted to see. "Sounds great."

I found the boot but then decided against it and put on black ballet flats instead. It was a little too cold for such reckless footwear, but I was going to dinner with Tobias . . . who could care about cold feet?

We turned the corner on Perry Street and then there we were, right at Hudson. A cute restaurant with a green awning and no more than ten or twelve tables. There were potted plants out front and a small wicker bench.

"I'll put our name in," he said.

I sat down on the bench. The wind in New York is worse than the weather. It zipped around me and I pulled my hunting jacket closer. I wished I had brought a hat. Or worn different shoes.

I watched him through the glass window talk to the hostess, a pretty twenty-something. He said something and she laughed, tucking some hair behind her ear. She nodded and Tobias moved toward the door, poking his head out to me.

"They can take us now," he said.

I felt, like the hostess, no doubt, charmed by him—by his magnetic charisma.

We walked in and sat down on the far side, by the kitchen. It was warm back there, and I shivered in the temperature reversal. "Toasty."

"Mm-hm." Tobias flipped over his menu. I already knew I wanted red wine and the scallops. They were seared in butter and served with a salad of mixed wild greens.

Instead, I studied Tobias. He was reading like he needed glasses. Holding the menu out, squinting. Between us, the tiny flame of the candle danced.

"Five," I said.

Tobias smiled, but he didn't look at me. We had been playing for a while now. A shorthand for intimacy. It had stuck, and now it had become about much more. A sort of thermometer—a way to check in on where we were at any given moment.

"Food," he said. "Wine."

"Duh."

His eyes flickered upward. "Cute," he said. He started studying me back. I felt my face get hot.

"Back at you."

He nodded. "Here."

"And."

"And." He set his menu down. He put both his elbows on the table. "I want to say something, but I'm not sure how you'll take it." He cleared his throat. He was nervous, I realized. He looked how I felt.

"Try me."

"Love," he said. He paused after he said it, looking at me. There was something so wonderfully open about his face. Even his features looked wider, like they had softened, spread out.

"Do you mean that?"

"You can't lie in Five," he said, his face still soft. "That's the number one rule."

My thoughts wanted control over my mouth. *It's only been a few weeks. It's too soon.* But what I said was, "Me too."

"Those are two words," Tobias said. His eyes crinkled up at the sides. I found him spectacularly beautiful.

"It wasn't my turn to play."

We leaned across the table, *Lady and the Tramp*–style.

The word I was thinking of wasn't *love*. If he had asked me right then I would have said something different. I would have said *lucky*. I was so lucky. I was lucky fate had taken such an interest in me. Me! Who was I to have such a story with the universe? But here he was, sitting before me. Living, breathing proof that my life was extraordinary.

"You act like being with him is winning some kind of prize," Jessica would say to me later—much later. "That's not what relationships are about."

But weren't they? Wasn't love about feeling like the luckiest woman on the planet? Wasn't it feeling like the whole world was conspiring for your happiness, and yours alone?

We didn't say "I love you" for another six months, but I didn't even notice. By that point the words were irrelevant. They only ever mattered in Five. And we always used *love*. Always.

Sometimes we'd tease it out. I'd say *like* a lot. We'd pretend we'd forgotten. But it was always there. The last, most important word.

It's fitting, then, that love was the last thing to go.

We had dinner that night. Scallops and linguini with clams in a lemon-oil sauce and the burger. We filled each other in on our pasts. More than we'd shared before. Tobias had grown up in Northern California. "I love the rain," he said. "Did I already tell you that?"

We wanted to be thorough. We wanted to make sure we left nothing out.

I told him about my father at that dinner. About how he'd left, about how he'd died not too long before. It felt important, so I told him. He listened without sympathy or judgment. Tobias was always profoundly good at that: listening. If I had a crappy day at work or got caught in the rain without an umbrella, Tobias would listen with the patience of a poetry professor. At first I loved it—he was so giving. But as time went on I found that I wanted him to talk more. It was like he thought it was enough to know me for the both of us, but it wasn't. I wanted to know what went on inside him, too.

9:23 P.M.

L OVE." I REPEAT IT AGAIN. The table falls silent. The clatter of plates even dims around us. A thirty-something lesbian couple has occupied the table where Tobias and I once sat, uttering this very same word. They're holding hands. I wonder if it's new, if something special will happen here tonight for them, too. The table with the champagne has settled into coffee and dessert. The people with the child have departed.

"Is a challenging word," Robert says.

Jessica leans over me toward him. "No," she says. "It's the easiest word in the world. Love isn't hard."

It's funny, I think, how she can vacillate so readily between the hopeless romantic of our early twenties and realist woman she's become.

89

Conrad and Audrey exchange a glance. He tilts his head toward her, encouraging her to speak for the both of them.

"Like I said, I never found love easy," Audrey says. "But then again, I don't think it was supposed to be."

I remember, now, once watching a documentary on Audrey Hepburn. She grew up in Germany during World War II. She was in hiding from the Nazis; her parents were sympathizers. She developed asthma due to poor conditions. I realize she's been coughing periodically throughout our meal. Did she always do that?

The documentary, a special on E!, I think, was titled *Audrey: The Pain Behind Perfection*. Not exactly an authoritative biography, but a fun way to spend two hours. Black-and-white reenactments were included, even if most of the details were wrong. The documentary surmised that she was modest about her EGOT awards, but she only received her Emmy and Grammy after she died. And it spoke of her rumored eating disorder, which was patently false. Her frame was a product of childhood malnourishment, not regimentation.

"What do you mean?" Jessica asks.

Audrey interlaces her fingers in front of her chin. Her delicate features sing out like stars, and I see that the lighting scheme in the restaurant has changed—we're operating on a lot more candles now.

"Fame came easy to me. Not understanding it, mind you, but having it."

"Important distinction." Conrad.

"I suppose. I think maybe in my heart I believed I could only have one. That certainly didn't help."

"Love or success?" Tobias asks.

"Oh, I think more like love and Audrey Hepburn." She twirls a gold ring around her middle finger. It doesn't look like a wedding band, but it might be. She seems like the kind of woman who would move it over, keep it close, change it into something else. Wear it as a reminder, maybe not even of him. "Being successful is so much about the self," she says. "Particularly in a profession where one must be the face of their product." She holds a hand up to frame her face. "This is me."

Conrad pats her shoulder. "Lovely, indeed," he says.

She waves him off. "I tried, but I could never figure out how to be what I needed to be for my career and simultaneously for a man. I wanted a family so much. It was the only thing that really ever mattered to me—I sacrificed a lot of my happiness in pursuit of something I believed would make me happy."

"But in the best relationships, that's the point," Jessica says. "You don't try and make each other weaker. You're not supposed to have to choose. You support each other."

Jessica all at once sounds very young. Naive, even. I can tell by the way her voice trails off at the end that she's heard it, too.

"That's true, Jessica," Audrey says. "But over time it is sometimes difficult to maintain. Maybe it was my era, too."

"Certainly couldn't have helped," Conrad offers.

Audrey drops her eyes to the table. I am concerned she is crying. The lighting is too low for me to tell. "For a long time I was wracked with guilt. I thought I could have tried harder, I could have done more." Her eyes meet mine. They are, in fact, saucer-wide and wet. "I don't want you to feel the same way. I don't want you to carry that."

Something so tender tugs at my heart as I watch her. "Can I ask you something?" I say. "All of you?"

"Absolutely," Conrad says. His hand hasn't left Audrey's shoulder and now he is offering a handkerchief from his inside pocket. She declines.

"Did I . . ." I'm not sure how to phrase this. "Did you have a choice? About coming here?"

"Oh," Audrey says at the same time Robert says, "Of course."

I look at Tobias. I know I'll find the answer there.

"A little of both," he says, which is as good as saying no.

"I think it was different for all of us," Audrey says.

"Well, I was always in," Conrad says. "I don't get back East nearly enough these days. Or see my old students. Or meet Audrey Hepburn." He winks at her.

Audrey flutters her hand. "Sh, sh. I don't think any of us have done something like this before." She looks at Robert. Her eyebrow is cocked in a gesture of impertinence. *Go on.*

"No," he says. "Never."

I all at once understand the implication here. He's never done it before, which means since dying he has only ever seen me. Since he's been gone he's never visited his wife or Daisy and Alexandra or met the new baby.

I see him sitting here, nervous, upright, and I know when this is all over, when they leave and go back, respectively, to wherever they came from, I will point to this as the first moment of softening. The first rounding of a once harsh corner.

Something has begun to change.

"Robert," I say, and he looks up at lightning speed. "What happened after you brought me home?"

His face registers a momentary surprise, like a flickering light, and then it settles on hesitant joy. It's strange to see, particularly here and now. I've asked him to tell me about the beginning of the end, how it happened, when he got sick, in what way he left, but on his face—the way his eyebrows arch up, up! The way his cheeks sink backward, away. Lips slightly parted. I may as well be asking him to read me a bedtime story. The one with the little girl who has a shit father who in the end, the final, magical moments, redeems himself. It doesn't seem impossible right now. It seems like it's maybe even something I might have heard before.

TEN

I T WAS A NASTY WINTER, the one Tobias and I lived through
right at the start of our relationship. Record number of snowstorms,
frigid-cold temperatures, the kind that make going outside, even for
an around-the-corner coffee, nearly impossible. Objectively, it was
bad. But when I think of it I can only remember the good. The cold
was cause for us to stay inside together. The snow days were stretches
of time in which we didn't need to get out of bed. We barely saw anyone else, and I barely noticed, if at all.

At the time, Tobias was working for a commercial photography
company called Digicam. He'd quit the job at Red Roof after Digicam had offered him a full-time photography gig. He'd been pounding the pavement for months, sending his résumé everywhere, and
finally someone bit.

It was commercial work, but they promised him they'd throw

him some "real" shoots—hard creative stuff—in between. He was thrilled. He'd finally have a chance to produce real work and get paid for it. But over time, their promise turned out to be empty—the job proved to be nearly all mass-market stuff—cleaning products, paper towel ads. He was hawking Fit Tummy Tea.

But the gig also wasn't particularly demanding, and in the beginning that was nice—it gave us plenty of time together. Tobias would come over on a Thursday and spend the weekend straight through. We ordered the requisite greasy pizza and Chinese and watched *24* on television in the living room when Jessica wasn't there—which was a lot. Jessica was mostly at Sumir's, but when she did hang out, it was always fun. She and Tobias were developing their own relationship, their own unique language. They'd e-mail each other articles about tennis or music, two things I couldn't keep up with the way they could. But mostly she wasn't there; mostly it was just the two of us. I am embarrassed to admit how fine that was for me. How much I didn't miss her.

Especially because now that she's gone, and that it has been her choosing and not mine, I miss her terribly. Not every day. Not constantly. But in moments when I come home and the apartment is dark, or when there is a great rerun of *Friends*, or a new episode of *The Real Housewives*, or I'll find a dried-up face mask in the back of my medicine cabinet—the missing stings like a slap. Not that she's *not* there, although I feel that, too. It's more that I can't call and tell her these things. I could, of course, but it would make it worse, because I know she doesn't care. The baby would cry and Sumir would shout, *Who is it?* and she'd say, *Sabby, what's up? I can't talk.* And the loneliness I'd feel from that particular interaction—her life so full, mine still so microscopic—all the same misfit details—would be enough to send me back to bed.

I introduced Tobias to David and Ellie during that winter. I wanted him to be a part of the fold.

"I don't know why he does it," Jessica said in regard to David on one rare night the six of us had gone to dinner. Tobias, Jessica, Sumir, and I were walking home from the East Village. Tobias and I had pushed the dinner three times. He never wanted to go out— *All I need is here with yo*u—and I wasn't one to argue, but Jessica had finally insisted.

"He deserves to be with someone who can love him in a real way."

"Maybe he doesn't want that right now," Tobias said. It was cold out, our breath was making short, fast-moving clouds in front of us. My fingers were numb. We had spent all our money on dinner, though, and besides we weren't far from the apartment.

"Everyone wants that," Jessica said. It was dismissive. Tobias shrugged it off, but I could tell it irked him.

"The last guy seemed nice," Sumir said absently.

"No, he didn't," Jessica said. "He seemed like all the rest."

"Maybe he's happy," Tobias said. He knew Jessica, knew that she was opinionated, that she liked things to be her way. He even joked about it with her. I was surprised when he pushed back.

"He's not," Jessica said, a little bit angrily. She was unaccustomed to being challenged, too. She didn't like it.

"Babe, you don't know," Sumir said. We glanced at each other. The two peacekeepers thrust into roles we didn't want.

David was Jessica's friend in college, but I suspected over time, as we moved to New York and life evolved, he had grown to like me more. He called me sometimes to make plans without her. Jessica could be intense. Her constant pursuit of self-improvement wasn't everyone's bag, I knew that. She'd want to have deep, intellectual talks in the back of dimly lit bars when other people didn't want to talk at all. She had sweeping ideas about love and life and she was still, in those days, talking in generalities. She hadn't yet been married, hadn't yet had a baby, hadn't folded to the practicalities of life. She liked to talk, which is maybe why I missed her so much in those first years without her—she left such a big, quiet space.

On the corner of Washington and Perry a man shouted Tobias's name. We turned around. A guy was jogging over—late thirties, maybe—dressed in a suit. Tobias smiled.

"Jeremy," he said. "No way." They exchanged a hug. "How have you been?"

"Good, work is wild. Irena is still traveling like a crazy person."

Jeremy looked to me, and Tobias slipped an arm around me. "This is my girlfriend, Sabrina," he said. I loved hearing him say *girlfriend*. I could have played it on a loop.

I held out my hand. "Nice to meet you."

"We're gonna take off," Jessica said next to me. We hugged and I waved good-bye to the two of them. Tobias was still engrossed with Jeremy.

"So how do you two know each other?" I said, turning back to them.

"Jeremy was my boss when I was at UCLA. We worked for Irena Shull. She did a lot of travel pieces. I was only an intern, but this guy let me come on shoots. He even convinced the magazine to fly me to Zimbabwe." Tobias smiled wide. "I can't believe you're still in that game, man."

He was lit up. I felt my stomach squeeze. I'd never seen him this animated talking about anything he was doing now.

"How about you?" Jeremy asked.

Tobias shrugged. "Working, which is good. It's not particularly stimulating, but life is good." He tugged me in closer to him and rubbed his thumb back and forth on my waist.

"We should grab a drink sometime. You still have my number?"

Tobias nodded. "Yeah, I'll hit you up."

Jeremy left, and Tobias and I started walking again arm in arm. "I didn't know you went to Zimbabwe to shoot. That's really cool." It sounded so silly. I was fishing for something, I just wasn't sure what.

"Well, I didn't shoot. But it was fun." He paused. "Jeremy's great. He's going to be a huge deal someday."

"So will you," I said.

Tobias spun me around and kissed me. "I love you," he said. "So much. I don't know what I'd do without you. You're it for me, Sabrina."

"Me too," I said. There weren't big enough words. I pressed my lips to his again, satisfied.

⚜

Jessica got married sometime later. The wedding was at the Central Park boathouse. It was beautiful, but it poured rain, and they couldn't take any pictures outside—something that visibly upset Jessica. She cried half her makeup off before the ceremony. The makeup artist kept running around with a blotting pad, muttering, "It's good luck."

David came and brought a *Vanity Fair* writer who *Refinery 29* had put on their Hot Single Men list three years running. He hadn't been invited with a plus-one and the events coordinator had to scramble for seating. Ellie didn't bring a date, but she had just started seeing a guy she'd met on JDate. He was a pharmacist. They stayed together for four years before she married his friend after the least-scandalous breakup ever. The ex even came to the wedding.

Jessica doesn't have any sisters, just much younger brothers, and I was her maid of honor. We'd gotten ready at the Essex House on Central Park South. I wore a lavender silk dress with a lace trim belt Jessica had picked out. She wore an ivory taffeta gown with a smat-tering of sequins at the waist. When I first saw her, standing there fully dressed, I teared up. She was so beautiful. She had on tiny sap-phire earrings that were her mother's and blue satin shoes that she kicked off midway through the dance party.

"You should get married every weekend!" Ellie sang. She was twirling to Robyn, and too drunk. That was the problem with throw-ing a wedding in your early or mid-twenties—no one was reasonable with an open bar.

Ellie was inches away from the DJ when Tobias caught her and spun her back toward the floor. The song changed to Sinatra, and I watched them sway together. From over the top of her curls, Tobias smiled at me, and my heart tugged at this—this man who loved me and was looking after my friend.

I gave a toast. In high school I had taken speech, and from that point on I liked speaking in public. I was good at presentations in college, and was comfortable pitching books to my bosses in meet-ings. But when I got up there and looked down at Jessica, I started shaking. There was too much I wanted to say. I couldn't fit it all.

"You're an inquisitive person," I had written to her. "You question everything. But you never questioned Sumir."

I said some more stuff then, about meeting her freshman year in the dorms, about her coming home to tell me she had met someone—

Sumir. I left off her bathroom-mirror quotes, even though I'd put them down in the speech. I'm not sure why.

We danced to Motown and Tobias and I shared a slice of carrot cake (Sumir's favorite) and afterward, when we were stuffed inside the twin room we'd rented at the Radisson on West Thirty-second Street (I can't quite remember why it seemed important to stay at a hotel when we had an apartment ten blocks south, but it did), Tobias asked me whether I thought never questioning was good.

"What you said in your speech," he said. "Do you think asking questions is a bad thing?"

I hadn't specified either way. When I wrote it, I had wondered how I felt about it. Is "just knowing" something that happens when you meet the right person? Or is it a personality thing? Do some people still constantly question?

But then I thought about it: I had questions with Tobias. Tons of them. But they never made me question how I felt about him. I knew he asked himself all sorts of things. Was he ever going to make it as a photographer? Would we ever make any money? Did he belong in New York?

I didn't want to think that meant something specific about us as a couple. I didn't want to think his questions ever ended in the rightness of me.

"I'm not sure," I said. "I think maybe different people do it different ways."

"Different people definitely do it different ways," he said. He seemed irritated. It wasn't an emotion I had ever registered on him before, and I felt my stomach bottoming out. Anger I had a framework for, but irritation seemed like a first step into something else—distaste, removal, maybe. With anger, there was heat, emotion. With irritation there was just distance. I wanted us to stay close, to stay sealed against each other. Our relationship seemed dependent on it.

"Is there something you want to say?" I asked. I remember thinking I could blame it on too much champagne if we argued. In the morning I'd wake up and roll over and kiss his neck and pretend like nothing had ever happened. If he asked, *Are you still mad?* I'd keep kissing him. *About what? Did we talk about something? I had way too much to drink last night.*

"I got offered a job in Los Angeles."

"What?"

Tobias rolled me on top of him. "I love you," he said. "That first, before we talk about anything else."

My head was spinning. *California?* "What is it?" I asked.

"Wolfe needs a new assistant."

I knew how much Tobias admired Andrew Wolfe. He was an up-and-coming Patrick Demarchelier, but more grunge. He mostly shot models or up-and-coming starlets in see-through gauze tops and underwear. It was art. I could see that. His pictures were ethereal—beautiful in the way the human body is—simple, perfect, nubile. But I knew the effect Tobias had on women. I had seen it since our first afternoon together.

We'd be eating at a café, and the waitress would fill his wineglass just a little bit higher. He was always getting touched. By baristas, women of all ages, gay men in my neighborhood. People gravitated to him like he was a twenty-four-hour diner at four A.M. It was like he had a neon sign above his head: OPEN.

I knew Tobias was slowly becoming ensconced in cement at his job. Day after day he took pictures of Windex and vacuums. The most exciting shoot he'd been a part of in months was for sugar. I didn't want that for him—I wanted him to follow his dreams. I just didn't want them to lead him away from me.

"Wow." That was all I could say. We'd been together for two years then. It felt like much longer.

"Jeremy?" I asked.

He nodded.

I hadn't even known he'd followed up with him.

"I can't turn this down," he said. "It's too big. It's the opportunity I need to do what I want." He touched my cheek. His fingertips were cold. "What if you came with me?"

I had just started my first job in publishing. I loved it, and I wanted to climb the ladder there. It was totally different from the designer. I felt like I was actually, finally good at something.

"I can't," I whispered. I thought if I opened my mouth too wide I'd start sobbing and never be able to stop.

"We'll figure it out," he said. He leaned his forehead down to mine. He was crying. "We have to."

We slept entwined in each other that night, but when we woke up the next morning everything had changed. We would fight constantly for the next ten days. Starting with: Why didn't he tell me sooner? It turned out he'd known about the job for two weeks.

"I didn't want to ruin the time we had," he said.

Be here now.

✦

I realize we've skipped ahead, but that's probably for the best. Consistent contentment so rarely makes for good storytelling.

In those two years in the beginning I was happy, and happiness has a way of quickening. Grief marks things. Joy lets them through. Days and months can pass in the blink of an eye. I was happier than I ever remember being in my life. Things changed. Jessica and I moved out. Tobias and I moved in. She got engaged. Then married. And then, he left. We were two years in, six since Santa Monica.

What I didn't know then was that we were only halfway there.

9:31 P.M.

T HE FIRST SIX MONTHS ARE THE hardest," Conrad says. "I remember when we took my daughter home, my wife would barely
let me touch her. All she did was cry." He motions to the waiter for
more wine. His cheeks are rosy, and he puts a hand to his chest when
he laughs.

"A whirlwind," Audrey adds. "Feedings and sleepless nights."
She looks sympathetically at Jessica, who nods.

"I'm out of that part, mostly." She hasn't quite recovered from her
previous embarrassment, I can tell. Jessica retreats fairly easily, but
she doesn't stay down long. I know she'll be back and engaged soon
enough.

"How old is the baby?" Audrey asks.

"Seven months," Jessica says. "Although he looks like he's two
years old." She looks at me to corroborate.

"It's true," I say. "He's big! And both his parents are so tiny."

Jessica laughs. "I don't know where he came from. Sometimes I tell my husband I had an affair with a linebacker."

When Jessica first started using the term *my husband*, I thought it was so crazy. We were just twenty-five, we were babies. The biggest thing I did was purchase a new Brita filter.

"But Conrad's right," Jessica says quietly. "I barely know where I am right now."

"We were happy," Robert says, steering us back. "You were the most beautiful baby either one of us had ever seen. Your mother used to say you looked like a little doll."

"She still calls me that," I say. *Baby doll*. I always figured it was just a term of endearment.

"Cabbage Patch Kid," Jessica says. "I can see it."

"Freckle face." From Tobias.

"You used to like them," I say. I'm being candid.

He raises his eyebrows at me. "Did I say freckles are a bad thing?"

Are we flirting? How is it always so easy to get back here?

Habits make of tomorrow, yesterday.

"You were beautiful," Robert says. He clears his throat. Takes a big gulp of water. "I was working. I made enough so that your mother didn't go back after her maternity leave. Things were difficult, but still okay."

Conrad adjusts his notebook in his pocket. Audrey keeps looking at Robert encouragingly. I can tell it's taking effort for him to continue.

"What happened was we got pregnant with another baby."

The table falls silent. Only Audrey says, "Oh dear."

"Mom never said that," I say, as if trying to prove him wrong. Another baby?

"She was excited, naturally. She was already three months when we found out. We weren't trying. You were three years old and a handful."

I'm looking at Robert, who appears older all of a sudden. Like he's not the age he was when he died, but the age he would have been had he lived.

"There was no heartbeat at the five-month checkup. It was a girl." The staccato sentences come one after the other. They seem to hit me straight in the chest like skipping stones. Not for what they lost, so long ago. But for the history I've been missing. The key passage torn out of the book.

"So you started drinking to numb the pain?" I ask. Because regardless, we still ended up here. That hasn't changed.

"We had all the usual issues a couple does when they go through something like this. I was already sick; I mentioned that. It's a lifelong disease. The circumstances just heightened it."

"That's understandable," Audrey says. I feel Jessica glare at her next to me, and I feel a rush of affection for my best friend.

"The thing that I regret is that I didn't realize what I did have. I lost sight of you. I was so busy mourning one thing, I forgot about the other."

I look down at my plate. My risotto appears cold and plastic, like the for-show plates that sit outside Italian restaurants in Little Italy. It makes my stomach turn just looking at it.

I feel a hand on my shoulder. I know it's Tobias's. I wonder if that ever fades. The feeling of his touch, like this. As if my skin is some kind of memory foam.

"She asked me to leave, but I would have gone anyway," Robert says. "After another year, she could barely stand to be in the same room as me. And I had turned into a monster."

"But you got help. After you'd already left us."

Robert closes and opens his eyes. "Shortly after, yes. I rented a small room at a motel. The woman who ran the front desk took a liking to me, bless her. She found me in the closet, high off heroin, three days after I checked in. By some miracle she got me into a clinic. I barely remember that time."

My sinuses start throbbing. I can feel them behind my eyes like hot pokers. This happens sometimes. I get brutal, debilitating headaches. When I was in college I would have to lie in a dark room for days, sometimes, with a cold compress on my face. They're better now, manageable, but there is never any telling when one might completely knock me off my feet. I pray it's not now.

"Headache?" Tobias says next to me. His tone has dropped, the decibel he used to use in the mornings when he'd bring me coffee or want sex. Sweet, languid. Like we had all the time in the world.

I press a thumb to my eyebrow and exhale the pressure. "I need some air," I say. If I have any hope of this not spiraling, I need to move.

I push back my chair and stand up. Conrad stands up, too. "I'll accompany you," he says. "Let's go outside."

I want to be alone, but I'm not sure that's an option, and anyway the way he says it, fatherly, authoritative, like a professor, which he is, makes me nod in agreement. I grab my bag to take with me.

"Are you sure you can . . ." Robert looks concerned. He knows we're not finished yet.

"Jessica went to the bathroom," Conrad says. "We're fine." And that's that.

Conrad holds open the door for me, and we step outside. The air is cold, and I wish I had brought out my coat. It hasn't snowed yet, but I get the sense it might. Not tonight, but soon. Holiday decorations are up. The city is in the jovial, neighborly phase it enters every year from Thanksgiving through New Year's. It can be the loneliest season, December in New York.

I pull my scarf around me. I stick my fingers in my bag and root around for the pack. I offer Conrad one. I didn't start smoking alone until Tobias left, and then I never stopped.

"What the hell," he says. "This can't possibly count."

We inhale and exhale together. Smoke fills the air around us.

"How are you doing?" Conrad asks.

His arms are crossed and he's looking at me with his head tilted. His lips shift side to side subtly and I have a wave of nostalgia for his class—the mentor I found nearly ten years ago.

"You know it was originally Plato," I tell him.

He raises his eyebrows at me like *go on.*

"On the list," I say, inhaling.

He nods, recognition dawning. "I would have liked to see that."

"Me too," I say. I laugh, and the smoke exits my lungs in a hurry.

"Why did you swap him out?" he asks.

"After class was over," I say, "I always felt like you had more to teach me." I want to add something more. Something about how he was a grown man who was there for me, and I'd never had that before, not really. Something about missing him, but I don't want it to come out wrong.

"So how are you doing?" he asks me after a moment. "I'm going to keep asking."

"Not so great," I say. I move my thumb back and forth from my temple to the top of my nose. I take another drag. Hold it. "I have a headache," I say through my exhale.

"Indeed."

"I get them sometimes," I say.

"I remember a particular midterm where you had taken to your sickbed for this very condition."

"Out of hundreds of students, you remember that?"

"I do," he says, chuckling.

"I was lying," I say. "I was so behind in your class. I missed half the lectures."

Conrad laughs. "Then what, might I ask, am I doing here?"

The smoke dances in the night air. "It wasn't about your class," I say. "I loved you."

I look over at him. He nods. He knows this. Conrad seems, all at once, to know everything. What has happened, how all this will end. So I ask him.

"What is going to happen in there?"

He taps some ash down. I watch it fall. "I think you will remember some things."

"Like that I love my father?"

"Maybe." He inhales. "It might help."

"It might hurt," I say. "He is, after all, dead."

Conrad laughs. It's another hearty belly laugh. "And?"

I look inside. Jessica is leaning over the table, showing her wedding ring to Audrey. Robert is saying something to Tobias.

"And."

If our relationship could be described in one word, it would be that. Never final. Never just this. Always *and* what if? *And* next. *And* after. There was always a sequel.

"I don't know," I continue.

"Now, that's not true."

Tobias leans over Robert. He pulls something out of his pocket. A watch. I take a step closer to the glass. Robert holds it in his hand. It's a gold pocket watch. I gave it to Tobias for his twenty-ninth birthday. It was my father's. It was the one thing I had of his, that he'd worn, and I gave it to Tobias. It was half compass, half watch. I remember saying to him: *So we can always find our way back.*

He brought it here tonight.

"We're not finished," I say.

Conrad takes another inhale and then snuffs his cigarette out on the pavement. He holds open the door. It's only nine-thirty. We have food still on the table. But that's not what I mean.

We're not finished. We're here to find our way back.

ELEVEN

TOBIAS LEFT TEN DAYS LATER. He moved out and into a beat-up Prius he had bought with a cash advance and drove out to California with three boxes of things I helped him pack. I even labeled them. *Clothes. Odds and Ends. Art.* He kissed me and said he'd call from the first stop. I told him not to. We'd gone back and forth about this over the last week. He wanted to stay together; I wanted to break up. It wasn't that I didn't want to be with him. Every cell in my body wanted to cling to his irrevocably. It was that I couldn't put myself through the kind of heartbreak I knew was waiting for me. When my father left, my mother changed our locks and that was that. I knew I hadn't escaped that particular programming. I didn't know how to do it differently. I had to cut the cord.

"You'll come visit next month and then I'll fly back the one after. We'll alternate."

I imagined the worst, on repeat. I'd call and Tobias wouldn't pick up and I'd see him on the beach with some bikini babe. I didn't think he'd cheat on me, but I didn't want to find out. If I ended it now he'd be free to do whatever he wanted in California, and maybe I could spare myself some pain. What I said to him was this: "Long distance doesn't work. If it's meant to be, it will be later."

"You don't believe that," he said. "Why are you doing this to us?"

He was right, I didn't. That was something Jessica would say, something she'd write in steam on the bathroom mirror. I subscribed more to *look out for number one*. After all, he was. He was leaving. I resented that he was trying to make me the responsible party.

"I do," I said.

He shook his head. "So come with me." He hadn't given up on that. It was his response daily. *Just come with me. Let's do this together. You'll get a great job there, too.*

"Stop," I said. "I can't. You know that. I have a career, too, remember? Publishing is a New York business."

"Of course I remember." He ran his hand through his hair. It was long then. A full head of curls. "But I want you with me. I want to be there for you. I want to sleep next to you and make you coffee in the morning and be in your life. This is one chapter. The next time, we can go where you need us to."

"I need us to be here," I said.

Jessica thought I was crazy. "You love him," she said. She was frantic. Up until the minute that I walked him downstairs, she was trying to convince me to change my mind. We were in my room, surrounded by a swirl of my things—discarded in the process of packing his. "You'll regret this, I know you will. Just stay together."

"I can't," I said. "Long distance never works." What I meant was: *I won't be left. I won't be left again.*

"You don't know that!" She threw a pillow down hard on my bed. "You found him. *Him.* Sabrina, I'm serious. Don't give this up."

But I did. I didn't go, and I never asked him to stay. Standing by his car, the summer sun reflecting off my tear-streaked face, the words coursing through my body until I was sure he could read them on my skin. All that came out was "Please." He thought I meant: *Just go, make it quick, don't ask me again.* What I really meant was: *Stay.*

He held me. We cried into each other's shoulders. I didn't know how to say good-bye, so I didn't.

I went back inside. I drew the blinds and I lay on the floor of my bedroom.

"I don't know how to be here for this," Jessica said. She was crying, too.

"So don't."

She left. She was due to leave on her honeymoon, and the following week I'd get texts from her periodically. *Cabana honey!* Of Sumir lounging on a chair by the ocean. *Honey-dewing.* A plate full of melon and plumerias. I knew it was her attempt at reestablishing normalcy, of taking a break from the fallout. I responded with the like. *Yay. Aww. Love.* We were both pretending.

In those first early weeks, my coworker Kendra was the only one I confided in. We had both been hired as editorial assistants and started within a month of each other. We were working at an imprint called Bluefire that published mainly children's books. Kendra was a life-long young adult fan, and this was her dream job. I was desperate to move into the nonfiction sphere, but everyone told me once you got your foot in the door, moving internally was much easier. Most of our days were spent scheduling meetings and reading from the stack of submissions our bosses got from agents. Kendra was all wide-eyed wonder, out to discover the next Harry Potter. We'd spend lunchtime in the conference room, swapping manuscripts and bagels and trying to find a stepping stone to what came next. I would have loved it if my heart wasn't completely shattered.

"You need to go out," Kendra told me. "You know the best way to get over someone is to get under someone else."

"What if you like being on top?" I asked.

Kendra's eyes went wide. "A joke! She lives!" Kendra held her belly, which was round and plump like the rest of her. She had straight black hair and the greenest eyes I'd ever seen, besides Tobias's. She wore glasses with black wire frames and men's button-down shirts. She brought Toblerones to work that her mom sent her by the dozen. I was always sugar high.

"I can't go out," I said. "It's only been two weeks." I hadn't heard from him since he'd arrived in California. But it was what I had asked of him, and he was respecting that. Living without him felt like a sword to the chest every minute on the minute. There were small things, like his forgotten socks I found in the hamper, or the Le Creuset pot we bought at a yard sale and cooked chili in all winter. The whole apartment made me think of him. The whole city did.

"A friend from college is having a party," Kendra said. "Harlem. Eight p.m. We can get a marg after work and head up. Stay for twenty minutes." She stood back and studied me. "Just so, you know, if you kill yourself I can say I tried."

We went. The party was small—ten people hovered around a love seat and beanbag chair. We drank warm vodka and ate Tostitos, and I stayed three hours. There was a guy there named Paul who worked in the design department two floors above us at Random House. He was short and laughed easily. At the end of the night, I let him kiss me. And then I let him date me for almost two years.

9:42 P.M.

CONRAD AND I ARE BACK INSIDE, and dinner is in full swing. Robert hasn't said anything else; we're still processing. But Conrad comes back boisterous—clearly infused with the night air.

"More wine, *mon cherie*?" he asks Audrey.

She nods, her cheeks red. Her eyes settle on him as he pours, and I think that maybe Audrey Hepburn is developing a crush on Professor Conrad. Crazier things have happened tonight.

I'm hyperaware of Tobias to my left. I need to figure out what went wrong, to sort through it so that we can find our way back to each other. I feel compelled to tell him, to have him in this with me, but I'm not sure it's time yet. I look over at him. He's cutting a scallop with his head down, the way I know he does when he's really considering something. Tobias was never great at multitasking.

"Hey," I say. Just so he can hear.

He looks up at me like he's astonished to see me there. "Hi. How are you?"

We both laugh. It's an insane thing to ask.

"This is so strange," I say.

"Is it?" he asks.

"Of course it is. We're sitting at a table with Audrey Hepburn."

"Oh." He turns back to his meal.

I keep my voice low. "What?"

"Nothing," he says. "I thought you meant us."

I swallow. "That too," I say.

He smiles at me. That smile that used to stop me dead in my tracks. That used to strip me of sanity and clothing in the middle of any fight. And I think maybe he knows, too. Maybe he thinks we're here to get back as well.

"The food is really something else," Conrad says a little too loudly. "Truly divine. Has anyone tried the pasta?"

Jessica waves her hand in the air. She's twirling some tagliatelle around her spoon. "So good," she says through a mouthful.

"We really should have done this before," Audrey says, and the whole table bursts out laughing. I think, for the first time, as I look around, that maybe this wasn't such a bad idea after all. That maybe something important can and will happen here tonight.

"Too true, too true," Conrad says. "Audrey, entertain us. It is mealtime, after all."

"With what?"

"You know, when you were little, your mother used to sing 'Moon River' to you?" Robert says, like he's just now remembered it. The rush in his voice is excitement.

"Is that so?" Audrey says.

"I love that song," Jessica says. "We danced to it at our wedding."

I remember Jessica and Sumir swaying to Shania Twain, but I don't say that now. I know she's not lying, not intentionally. Jessica, for all her judgment and opinions, doesn't have the best memory.

"That was our favorite," Tobias says. Under the table I feel him reach for my hand. He squeezes once and then lets go. But the contact has been made. My whole body feels like a sparkler.

"Sing for us," Conrad says.

Audrey blushes. "Oh, no, no. I couldn't. There are people around."

"Nonsense," Conrad says. "They don't mind."

He stands up and claps his hands together. The restaurant falls silent. Waiters pause, mid-serve. Conversations halt. Wineglasses are suspended in hands mid-sip.

"Would it trouble anyone if my dear friend Audrey here sang a little tune?"

As if on cue, everyone swings back into motion. Sounds rush back in around us and people return to their meals.

"See?" he says. "It's no bother."

Audrey pauses. I can see she's considering it. And I hope she says yes. I want to hear her sing. It feels important, somehow. Her presence here is not just levity but something else, too. Audrey, for me, represents a time in which things were better. My parents together and Tobias and I—happy and in love.

"I'll be off," she says. "I haven't done it in so long."

"Just give it a go," Conrad says. He squeezes her shoulder in a gesture of support.

And then she begins. Her voice is angelic, no more than a whisper, but it's somehow richer and more authentic than it was in the film, or in the recording I have in my iTunes. I get the feeling that the people surrounding us can't even hear. It's like as soon as she begins we're on our own island at sea.

"Moon river, wider than a mile . . ." As she sings I am transported to a time many years before this one—before Tobias or Jessica or Professor Conrad. It's just me and Robert and Audrey. Her voice, its own memory. There is silence when she finishes, like a cloud of something delicate, spun cobwebs or gold, hangs over our table. Even Conrad seems at a loss for words. It's Robert who speaks first.

"That was wonderful," he says. "Thank you."

She reaches across the table and takes his hand, and I see that, for the first time in my life, my father is crying. We are split open in the wake of Audrey's voice, every one of us. What will flow into the cracks we do not yet know.

TWELVE

THE RELATIONSHIP WITH PAUL WAS FINE. Nice, even. I knew he was more invested than I was, but he never really showed it. We saw each other twice during the week and once on the weekends. We followed this rhythm week in and week out—never more, rarely less. I met his parents, but only because they happened to be in town and he had tickets to a Mets game. He didn't cook, and neither did I, so we ordered in. We liked the same television shows and slept in on Sundays. He told me he loved me after seven months, at the Italian place on Carmine we went to regularly. I said it back.

Occasionally I heard from Tobias. He'd send me e-mails with links to articles I might like—never to his own work. I responded back a line or two. "Thanks" or "I like this" or "I hope you're doing well." We didn't ask questions.

I had dinner with Matty a year in. He had texted asking if I wanted to get together. I had only seen him once or twice since Tobias left, and I missed him—he'd been my friend, too.

We met at the Indian place close to their old apartment we had gone to many times. Tobias obviously didn't live there anymore, and neither did Matty, but we met there anyway. A pilgrimage to our past. He came in carrying a copy of *Rolling Stone*.

We ordered chicken curry and yellow lentils and saffron rice, and once we'd eaten a bit I asked about Tobias.

"He's doing really well," he said. He spoke quietly, like he was trying not to startle me, gauging how I'd take it. "I think the work stuff is really good."

He didn't mention any woman, and I was grateful. I wasn't sure I could have handled that.

"I know he'd kill me if I told you," Matty continued. "But I wanted you to see."

He handed me the copy of *Rolling Stone*, which had been sitting on the table through dinner like a gun on the mantel. On the cover was President Obama. I opened it and went to the dog-eared page, which was the cover feature.

"You're kidding," I said.

"It's Wolfe's credit," Matty said. "But Tobias shot the whole thing."

My heart swelled with pride and then tightened with sadness because he hadn't told me. This was the thing he wanted most in the world, and I couldn't be there to share in it with him. A thought crossed my mind: that we could have the things we wanted, just not together.

Matty sensed my emotion. "How's Paul?" he asked. I remembered he'd met Paul at my birthday party a few months back and liked him.

I cleared my throat. "Good," I said. It was true. "We're going to Portland next week."

We were going to stay for a long weekend, explore the city and do some hiking. We already had all our dinner reservations.

"Nice," he said. "I love it there."

"I've never been, but Paul says I will, too."

I looked down at my food. Matty reached across the table and touched my arm.

"Hey," he said. "You know I thought you guys were totally meant to be, but maybe it's for the best, you know?" He swallowed. "He's doing really well, and I think you are, too."

I thought about work, my relationship. "Yeah," I said. I touched the magazine on the table. "This is amazing. Obama. Wow."

Matty grinned. He looked so proud. "Pretty cool. He's doing Harrison Ford next week."

After my dinner with Matty I thought about Tobias less and less. Knowing he was doing well, that he hadn't moved for nothing, that we'd gone through this for a reason, helped. I liked Paul, maybe I even loved him. I was happy. I was just starting to believe that maybe it *had* been for the best when Tobias came back. It was Christmas. He had been gone in L.A. for twenty-three months and six days when he showed up at my apartment.

I was renting out the second bedroom to a girl named Rubiah who was getting her doctorate in physics at Columbia and was never there. It was easy rent, and I liked the occasional company.

I don't know why he expected to find me there, but he did. I hadn't gone home with Paul. My mother and stepfather had elected to go on a cruise for the holidays. She asked me along, but I get seasick. People with migraines should never set foot on boats. So I decided to spend the holidays alone.

I baked macaroni and cheese and made cookies. I was just settling down to watch a History Channel special Rubiah had DVR'd about the end of the Mayan calendar. It was 2014, and they were claiming the end hadn't been in 2012 like expected, but was still coming.

He rang the buzzer. I heard his voice. "Hey," he said. "It's Tobias. Can I come up?" Just like that. *Hey, it's Tobias. Can I come up?* Like the world wasn't ending. Like it hadn't already.

I waited for him in the doorway. My heart pounded so loudly it was preventing me from seeing. He took the steps two at a time. He always did. He showed up with a bag. "I just got off the plane," he said.

It should have taken more. It should have taken explanation. Dates, times, plans. We had barely spoken in those twenty-three months. Not once in the last seven. But all I asked was: "How did you know I'd be home?"

"I took a shot," he said.

He put his hands on my face. I didn't even try and fight him. "Merry Christmas," he said.

"Why are you here?" I said.

"It's where you are," he told me.

"You shot Obama," I said.

He raised his eyebrow at me. He was smiling. "I believe Obama is fine and at the White House," he said.

I shook my head. "I thought you were doing great."

"I was," he said. "But it wasn't enough without you."

All I knew was that I missed him. Just seeing him there, standing where Paul had stood so many times in the last two years—coming, going, never hesitating—it was everything that I had been missing. It felt like my life for those last two years had been a silent black-and-white movie, and here he was rushing in with sound and color—making the whole thing come alive. He was my destiny returned.

I kissed him, because I wanted to know that he was real. That he wasn't some apparition. I had, at times, imagined a reunion exactly like this.

"Macaroni," he said, his mouth still on mine.

I resented how confident he was. But it felt like confidence in me, in us. It wasn't just his confidence that I'd take him back. It was my confidence that he had come back for me.

"Are you staying?" I asked.

"If you'll have me," he said.

That was all I needed. It sounds ridiculous. When it's isolated it seems like the most clichéd quote in the book. But there you go.

He dropped his bag in the entrance. He brought me in close to him. We started making out against the closet door. I wound my hands up into his hair—dirty. I felt his move down my back. I'd had sex with Paul for almost two years and hadn't felt, in all that time, what I did now, fully clothed, with Tobias.

He angled me toward the living room and then lifted me up and carried me into my bedroom. He knew the apartment. It had once been ours. It was ours again, maybe, already.

He laid me down on the bed and undressed me. I was hungry for him, impatient—all at once ravenous—but he took his time. He peeled off his shirt and hovered over me. He was tanner than he had been a few years ago, and heavier—denser somehow. I looked up at him.

"I waited for you," I said. As soon as I said it I knew it was true—I had. Paul, the apartment, the past two years—they weren't real. None of it had felt like waiting. It had all felt like the slow slog of moving on. But I had been wrong. I had been struggling against a current that had, all this time, been trying to tow me out to sea. Finally, I let it.

He kissed me, and I reached up and grabbed on to his shoulders. He moved his lips to my neck and I shifted under him as he slid his hand down to rest in between my legs.

The touch of his fingers sent me pulling at whatever clothing remained between us. It had been too long.

"Now," I said.

He pressed into me and we both exhaled sharply at the same time. He stopped inside me, unmoving.

"I missed you," he said.

"I missed this."

We started moving together. The rhythm of our bodies, the way he knew exactly how to touch me, what my nonverbal cues were. I felt heady, weightless, like I might spontaneously combust at the intensity of being close to him.

"Sabrina," he whispered softly. And all I could think was my name, my name, my name—over and over again. I was found.

Later, wrapped around each other in bed, I told Tobias about Paul. He listened intently as I filled him in. The party, the last nearly two years. He wasn't jealous; he was Tobias—thoughtful, honest, sincere.

"Do you want to end it?" he asked me.

"Yes," I said. I kissed him again.

I broke up with Paul the following week. When he was back in town I asked if we could get coffee. We went to this depressing Starbucks on Fifty-seventh Street that was kid-filled and loud. I got there first. I wanted to pick the table.

I ordered a whole-milk misto for him and a small coffee, black, for me. I think he knew already. Usually when he greeted me he was smiling. Life for Paul was like the chorus of a song. Familiar and melodic. Never any pivotal moments. No inspiring crises.

But he knew what coffee meant.

"What happened?" he asked me when he sat down, after thanking me for the coffee. Paul was very polite.

I thought about telling him I didn't think we were a match. That I wasn't where he was. And those things were true, sure. But they still weren't the answer.

"He came back," I said.

Paul knew enough about Tobias. In the beginning, he caught me crying. After sex, sometimes, which made us both feel pretty awful.

"I see." He said a lot of things afterward. About how Tobias would leave again. About how Tobias didn't deserve me. But none of his arguments were trying to convince me to stay. It didn't feel like he was campaigning for us. He already knew there wasn't much worth fighting for.

I didn't blame him. He only knew the worst of Tobias. Half truths and some complete fictions concocted in the heart of someone who was heartbroken. The real flesh-and-blood man was nothing like the fractured image Paul had in his mind. I couldn't hold his distorted picture against him. And of course, plenty of it was true, too.

I left the Starbucks and called Tobias. He came uptown and met me. When he saw me standing by the door he put his arms around me. "I'm sorry," he said. That was all. I let the *sorry* extend out. I let it blanket the whole last two years.

We went home, ordered in dosas, and ate on the floor. We were twenty-seven. At the time, it felt close to thirty. But now, here, it seems far closer to twenty.

We had twenty-four months left. The clock was on. But I didn't know it. There, in the dead of winter with him, it felt like the start of forever.

9:48 P.M.

T IME IS DOING THIS STRANGE THING right now. We're finishing our dinner. Sharing bites. Jessica passes some pasta to Audrey, who trades her for a scallop. The wine has sunken things into a casual intimacy, but for the first time since we sat down, I feel the immediacy of tonight. The need to solve and rectify what I must before the clock strikes what, midnight? Whenever it is that we will get up from the table and go our separate ways.

"You still have the pocket watch," I say to Tobias at the same time Jessica asks, "Why am I here?"

I'm so caught off guard by the question that I turn away from Tobias. "What do you mean?"

Jessica tears off a piece of bread and soaks it in sauce. "I know the list; I was there when you made it. I wasn't on it. I mean, I live forty-five minutes away, barely. You could see me anytime."

Nearly two years ago, I crossed out my grandmother's name and wrote in Jessica's. It was born out of anger. I still had the Post-it—tattered and curled at the edges. A reminder of the Jessica who used to be there, who used to fill our living room with papier-mâché and *her*.

Jessica isn't used to this much alcohol and I see the telltale signs of her wine-honesty. Cheeks pink. Eyes slightly unfocused.

"Because I could see you, but I never do."

Jessica sets down her fork. "That's not fair."

Jessica and I didn't have a falling-out—I still think of her as my best friend. There was no big fight, no disagreement. But sometimes it feels like something so irrevocable happened between us, and the fact that I can't put my finger on *when* makes it worse. If there was a fight, we could make up, apologize, recover. But you can't say sorry for a slow dissolve.

"But it's true," I say. "You're always too busy. When was the last time you were even in the city?"

"I have a baby," she says.

"You were too busy way before Douglas."

Jessica has this "out of sight, out of mind" mentality. In moments throughout our friendship she has expressed to me, always prompted, that it didn't mean she loved me any less. "I forget," she told me. "But it doesn't mean I don't need or care about you."

We barely have a real friendship anymore. I think the last time I saw her was three months ago, at Douglas's baptism. She has a seven-month-old baby whom I've only met twice.

"Since you moved out of our apartment," I say. "It's like you disappeared into the atmosphere. You never call me. You say I'm your best friend, but by what standard?"

"Were you there?" She turns to face me, all of her. I see, for a moment, the woman I used to know at twenty-two. Who was passionate and alive. Who would write *You are today* in lipstick on the tile of our kitchen floor. "You were so caught up with Tobias. I moved out, but you moved on, too. You were barely there when I was planning the wedding. And I didn't blame you. I wanted you to be happy. I still do."

"But I'm not," I say. "I haven't been."

Across the table, I see Audrey lean forward, but Conrad nudges her gently back.

"You still think I can fix it for you," Jessica says quietly.

"I don't think you can fix it." My lip has started to tremble. I know she knows I am about to cry. She knows all my tells, just like I know hers. "I just want you to still want to try."

And that's it, right there. The thing that hurts the worst. Not the action, of course not. Not the missed dinners and calls. Not the rescheduled plans. But the ache, deep down, that she no longer wants things to be any different than they are. That she's so immersed in her life she never thinks about what it's like to be in mine.

"More wine?" Audrey offers. I see her standing next to me, holding the bottle. She must have wriggled out of Conrad's grasp lightning quick. She puts a hand on the top of my head, and the gesture is so maternal that for a moment it's too much to bear. Audrey isn't that much older than I am, here wherever we really are, and yet it's like she's compressed her whole life down into this body. She's sixty and twenty-three and seventeen, all at once.

She fills my glass. She pours for Jessica and Tobias, too.

"I'm sorry," Tobias says slowly.

"This isn't about you," I say.

"You can't fix it," Jessica says to Tobias. "I can't, and you can't, either. Why are you here? Why did you come tonight? I love you, Tobias, but you're making it worse, you realize that, right?"

"I'm trying," Tobias says. I feel something cheer in my heart. He knows what has to happen here tonight. He wants to find his way back, too. To rectify what went wrong and start over again.

"No," Jessica says. "You're not. You're here and you're talking about things and you're remembering things, and what do you think is going to happen?"

"Why does that have to be a bad thing?" I ask her. "Why can't we go back and fix what went wrong? Isn't that why we're here?"

"You don't understand anything," Jessica says. "And I've already been the one to explain it to you too many times."

"Explain what?" I ask. "That we're not living up to your standards of a relationship? That if I get back together with him you won't be there this time to pick up the pieces?"

"No," Jessica says. She looks into her wineglass, like maybe she expects to find the answer there.

"Please," Tobias says. "Jessica." There is a warning to his voice. It sounds, all at once, completely unfamiliar.

"I'm sorry," Jessica says. She looks at me, and her eyes are wet, wide. "Tobias is dead."

THIRTEEN

F OR FIVE MONTHS, RUBIAH, TOBIAS, and I lived together. Rubiah and Tobias got along. She was rarely there, but on the occasion she was I'd come home to find them drinking beers or playing a board game. Matty had gotten Tobias into Risk years ago, and sometimes the two of them still met at Uncommons in the West Village to play together.

Rubiah's like of Tobias was cozy, and convenient, and allowed me to miss Jessica a little bit less. She was happy when Tobias came back—I knew she had wanted us to make it work the first time—but she was married now, and as time went on more and more judgmental, I thought, about choices that were different from her own. She had grown up faster, faster than Tobias and me, certainly, faster than any friends I knew. She was playing house now, and the realities of twenty-something life, the roller coaster I often felt like I was on—it seemed like she had skipped that altogether. So we lived with Rubiah, and it worked. But our updated *Three's Company*, if you could call it that, was short-lived. In the summer of 2015, Rubiah got a place up by Columbia, and Tobias and I decided to move, too.

I had been at that apartment on Tenth Avenue since the beginning, almost five years, and I was equally as sick of it as I was in love with it. I loved how much had happened there. How Jessica and I had moved in with nothing more than two suitcases apiece and a box of books mailed from school. The memory of our first Ikea trip, convincing our super to rent us a car because we weren't yet twenty-five. Scooting Jessica through the aisles on the pull cart, arguing over whether to get a sofa or two club chairs (we settled on a love seat and one chair). The late nights watching *Friends* reruns and that first year when Jessica used to wake up before me and go to the corner deli and get us both coffee—hazelnut creamer and one Splenda.

But I hated the rust-rotted sink, and how the bathroom flooded every time the upstairs neighbors took a shower, and how noisy it was with our street-facing bedrooms. I was ready for something else in the way you're ready to move from middle school to high school. Not because it's a personal choice, necessarily, but because it's time.

Tobias and I found a one bedroom on Eighth Street between Sixth Avenue and MacDougal. It was small and old, the stove rusted and the walls cracked despite a fresh coat of paint. But our bedroom faced the back and was relatively quiet. It was the third apartment we saw, and we took it on the spot.

Tobias had gone out looking when I was at work. He'd wanted to move to Brooklyn, but I'd won out. I felt certain that I didn't want to leave Manhattan, and Tobias relented. He didn't even really fight me on it. I think he knew he didn't stand a chance.

"This is the one," he'd said when he called me.

I checked the time: 11:38 A.M. "Is this the first place you've seen?" I asked.

"It's perfect," he said. "Trust me."

I snuck out half an hour later for lunch and met him on the front stoop. He had a bouquet of sunflowers. It was the season. "Welcome home," he said when I got there.

We went upstairs together (six flights), and as soon as I stepped inside I saw that he was right. It wasn't that it was perfect, not by a long stretch, but it was ours. Tobias was excited. "We can paint the living room," he said. "Maybe yellow." He snuck his hands around my waist.

"It's great," I said. "How much?"

He squinted at me. "Twenty-four, but I figure that's only three hundred over budget, right? And the broker said she'd cut her fee in half for us." He shrugged. For a brief moment I imagined some leggy brunette with a briefcase in our apartment, rubbing up against Tobias on the kitchen counter.

I didn't have the heart to tell him our budget was already two hundred over what we could realistically afford. I wanted that yellow living room, too.

Matty helped us move. He'd borrowed his father's van, which he lined with blankets. Tobias had sold his Prius in L.A. Matty was out of school then and working for a bank. "Overpaid and overstimulated," was how Tobias described Matty at his new gig. "He's like a puppy in heat."

"He's excited," I said. We were stacking boxes. Tobias gingerly set a lamp on the floor. Matty was downstairs, watching the double-parked van.

"Nah," he said. "He'd be excited if he were doing his own thing. He's just running full-blast on a hamster wheel."

Tobias chided Matty for not holding out for a start-up gig, or not developing an app on his own. He thought he was selling out. But Matty was twenty-three years old. "First money, then independence," he said whenever Tobias brought it up.

To me, Matty seemed happy, but by this point I understood Tobias's complicated relationship with success, money, and working for other people. He had done it in L.A., and he had enjoyed it—but only because he found the work to be creative, and important. He was a true artist—commercial success wasn't the point; often it was problematic. More than once I heard him tell Matty he'd stopped listening to a band after they'd made it. "The sound changes," he'd said. "It stops being pure."

He hadn't parted ways well with Wolfe (quitting wasn't part of the gig), and he was now working for one of Wolfe's rivals in New York—a practice, he said, that was all too common. He wasn't traveling as much, which I loved, and he was fine with it. Most of the shoots they did were for big ad firms in the city. It was a step down in sexy, but not as bad as the Digicam days, and the pay was decent, it was a job, and we were together. I knew he wasn't entirely happy with work, though, and it nagged at me. My defense of Matty often felt like a way to quell my guilt about Tobias—*It's okay to grow up.*

I stood in the small, wood-floored apartment as Matty and Tobias took turns running up and down the stairs with boxes. I played director. "To the left." "In the bedroom." "By the far wall." We had too much stuff for this tiny place, which was, all in, about a third of the size of our old apartment. Things had accumulated over the years.

Old chairs and throw pillows and small stools purchased at thrift stores on Second Avenue. Prints picked up on New York City sidewalks. Odd Ikea furniture (is it a TV stand or a desk?). Kitchenware caught between Tupperware and frying pan. Rubiah took little, and Tobias couldn't throw anything out (what if we needed that second egg beater?). It was a strange trait of his—out of character—this need to hoard. I tried to suggest cuts, but the move was stressful enough, so most everything made its way over.

Except, strangely, the photograph of his I had bought all those years ago. The tribal man. I couldn't find it anywhere. Not in the boxes when we unpacked, not misplaced in with the toilet articles, or stuffed in a bag of clothes. As the days went on and we broke down the boxes and stacked the dishes in the kitchen, I started to panic. I stopped by the old apartment—no one had seen it. I called Matty to check the van—nothing. I sat down on the bedroom floor one week after move-in and stuck my head, for the twentieth time, under the bed.

"Give it a rest," Tobias said. He had seemed less than curious about where it had gone. It occurred to me that maybe he had gotten rid of it.

"I can't," I told him. "It's the first thing I have of you."

"Who cares?"

"It was there in the beginning," I said.

"So were we."

"You're kidding, right?"

Matty was in the kitchen, trying to make a meal of condiments. We'd ordered pizza every night that week; I was sure we would again. Tobias took me in his arms. "Who cares about a photograph when I have you?"

"You never liked it," I told him.

He went back to arranging books on the shelf. "It wasn't my favorite, and I had better work. I was nineteen years old. I sucked."

He didn't understand. Who cared about the quality of the work? The point was the story. It was our bread crumb, maybe even our grail. I couldn't lose it. I felt, for some reason, like losing it would mean something significant for our relationship—some bad omen. Like the photograph was our lucky charm and without it we'd be doomed.

"Did you get rid of it?" I asked. "You can be honest with me."

"No," he said. And left the room.

That night, one of the first in our new place, I couldn't sleep. I kept thinking about the photograph, about where it could be. About how, of all the things we moved over, all the useless, random appliances and furniture, that had to be the thing to go missing. I had been so careful with it. I took it down and wrapped it in that same paper—the sheets that had housed it for two years. I folded it and locked it with tape. What had happened to it?

Tobias snored next to me, unconcerned. His head was on my chest and his curls tickled my neck. I thought about the boy who had taken that photograph. Who I had gone to see all those years ago. I didn't find him then, but I found that photo, and for all the things I didn't have, I still had that. Or had. That grainy man. I wondered if I had been holding on to the wrong thing.

9:52 P.M.

TOBIAS IS DEAD." NO SOONER HAS Jessica said it than I feel the crunch of metal through my body, the press of steel, the pounding pounding pounding of the cement chewing up my skin. When Tobias was hit, I felt it all, every last cracked rib and drop of blood. I've been trying to forget it happened. But of course it had. He's gone.

Stupid. Stupid stupid stupid stupid stupid.

Jessica is looking at me curiously, like she's not sure what my reaction will be. Like I may overturn the table. I won't, of course. It's not like this comes as a surprise. He's dead, I know. I was there.

Conrad is wearing a look of concern, and Audrey keeps repeating "Oh dear" under her breath. Robert says nothing.

"I'm sorry," Tobias says. "I'm so sorry. I thought tonight—"

"What?" Jessica interrupts, the fire in her voice back. "That you could turn back time?"

For some reason, at that moment, we all look at Conrad. Maybe it's that he's a philosophy professor, maybe it's that he's been the authority at this table thus far. But I think it's something else, too. Why are we here? How did this happen?

He holds up his hands as if to keep us at bay.

Audrey steps in then. "I think maybe we need a moment to digest this news."

Jessica digs the heels of her palms into her forehead. "With all due respect, we've been digesting this news for the last year."

The reality of his death crashes over me, the way it has so many times before. Those first few weeks, waking up gasping for air. The bolt of ice every morning realizing it wasn't a dream, this is my reality, he's gone.

And yet for the first time in a year I feel a seed of something different, something bright, new. Because maybe . . .

I reach for Tobias's hand under the table, and this time I don't let go, I hold it there. I feel his fingers curl through mine, the cool press of his palm. This is what I've been missing. This. Him. Flesh.

I know Audrey isn't coming back, or even my dad, but Tobias can. Tobias is mine. If it weren't for our mistake, if it weren't for what went wrong, he'd still be here. It's my job to fix this.

"What if that's why we're here," I say. My voice is shaky and I see my hesitation reflected on the faces of my dinner mates.

"I don't know . . ." Robert begins.

"No," I say. This is it, it has to be. I feel like I've stumbled on the key. I'm not interested in another point of view. I want to take

Tobias's hand and lead him out of here, away from all these nonbe-lievers. "That's what we're doing here tonight. We're going to be able to change things."

"Sabrina," Audrey says, and it's the first time she's addressed me by name. "I do not think that is such a wise notion."

"Why not?" I'm feeling defiant, wild. Because what else matters, really, other than having him back? "You said yourself we're here to figure out what happened." I turn to Conrad.

"I did," he says. "I didn't say change it."

"Maybe you can make peace," Robert says. "I know it sounds—"

"No," I say. "Stop, please, all of you." Their voices feel harsh, loud, like the cement drilling outside the apartment on Tenth at seven A.M. on a Saturday. I want it to stop.

I look to Tobias, and his eyes are filled with the kind of hope I feel, and I drop down into that—that shared space between the two of us. The place we resorted to time and time again over the last ten years—where we needed only each other. The one that smoothed over our toughest moments, that drew us back together.

"We can try to change, can't we?" Tobias says.

"I can't stay for this," Jessica says. "I can't. I can't see you . . ." She stands, and then Audrey stands, too.

"Sit down," Audrey says.

Jessica looks taken aback. She pulls her blazer more tightly around her. "I will not."

"I said sit down," she repeats, even more forcefully this time. Conrad puts a hand on Audrey's arm. "This is Sabrina's dinner, you remember? Jessica, please."

Jessica shakes her head. Then she plunks back into the chair. "That's easy for you all to say. When it doesn't work, I'm the only one who's going to have to stick around. You'll all go back, but I'll have to hear about how it didn't work, how it feels like she lost him all over again. . . ." Jessica's voice cracks, and she sucks in her bottom lip.

"Jess," I say. I'm still holding Tobias's hand. "I'm sorry; I have to."

"You want me to just sit here?" she says. She wipes the back of her hand against her face.

"No," I say. "No one here knows me as well as you do."

"That's not true," she says. "He does."

"No," I say. "He doesn't."

Tobias and I knew each other in big ways, sweeping ways, ways that felt eternal and unchanging. Fate. Destiny. The current of life pulling pulling pulling. But in the minutiae, in the day-to-day, in the coffee and poppy-seed bagel and *Friends* reruns and ballpoint over felt tip, it's her. She's always been my in-case-of-emergency person. I never wrote Tobias's name down. It was always Jessica.

"Please," I say. "I need you. And I need you to stay."

She looks at me. Her eyes tell me that she's tired, that she doesn't want to do this, that she knows it's a mistake, that we'll never figure our way back out. But she nods. "Fine," she says. "It's your dinner."

I feel Tobias's hand squeeze mine.

Conrad clears his throat. "You were telling us about how he came back from L.A.," he says.

"We were happy," I say. I pause, because for the first time I don't just want to relive my experience, I want to hear his, too. I want to know what this was like for him, all of it. "Weren't we?"

Tobias looks at me suddenly, almost violently. "Of course," he says. "How can you even ask me that?"

"Many things can be true at the same time," Jessica says.

FOURTEEN

T HAT SUMMER AFTER HE CAME BACK, when we were living on Eighth Street, rivaled our first year together for our happiest stretch of time. We rode around the city on bikes, ate ice cream from Big Gay on the High Line, spent whole afternoons on a blanket under the shade of a tree in Prospect Park. When I look back on it now, it's as if we were alone in the city, but of course that wasn't true. I had my job, and I was starting to find that children's publishing might be where I belonged. I had pushed for a middle-grade manuscript about an eleven-year-old Anne Hathaway, Shakespeare's wife, that my boss had bought and fast-tracked. I felt like maybe I had a knack for it.

Matty was dating a grad student at the New School, a writer by the name of Beth Sterns, and the four of us spent a lot of time together. She had an odd obsession with sunflower seeds. She was never without them. Subways, museums, even restaurants. There was a trail of shells wherever she went. She was nice. Whip-smart, too. Matty was still at the bank and was now considering a turn at a hedge fund, a pivot Tobias was, of course, against. But he had begun to share his thoughts less and less with Matty. "He doesn't want to hear it," he'd say after voicing a concern.

"I know he's disappointed in me," Matty said to me one night in August. We were in the kitchen of Matty's apartment, a new place in Midtown with sleek appliances and a wide view. He held the trash bin up as I shoveled empty takeout containers into it. Beth and Tobias were in the living room, setting up a board game.

"He's not," I said. "You know Tobias, he has impossible expectations."

Matty nodded. "It's not like he's out there on his own. He's doing ads for air freshener."

I winced. I hated being reminded of the reality of Tobias's career. The one where he was sacrificing his artistic merit to be here, to be with me.

"I worry about him sometimes," Matty said. Some curry had gotten on my hand, and I went to the sink to run water over it and to put some space between Matty and me. We were still in that perfect summer. I didn't want to know what he saw. The dinner I'd shared with Matty nearly two years ago flashed in my mind. How proud he'd looked. How he'd told me that maybe it was for the best.

"He's good," I said, my back still turned. "The job is temporary." I believed that it was. Tobias was too talented. Something else would come along, and this time, it would be here. I shut the water off. "Beth is great."

The pivot was not lost on Matty, who sighed deeply and handed me a dish towel. "Yeah," he said. "She is. Kinda wish she'd switch to almonds, though." We both laughed.

Matty and I went back to the living room. Tobias had joined Beth, and the two were black-toothed and grinning.

My friend Kendra, at work, was doing even better. She hadn't yet found the next Harry Potter, but she had brought over a British series by an author who had previously (and famously) refused to publish in the States. She had been promoted on the spot for it to Associate Editor. She had an office now, and although I missed her in the bullpen, the office came in handy for us.

It was a Thursday. Kendra and her boyfriend had a summer share in the Hamptons—or rather, he did. Our publishing salaries barely covered rent, let alone a beach house. She was dating a finance guy named Greg who seemed like an odd fit for her—I had met him, once, at a work BBQ our boss hosted at her house in Westchester, which had a proper backyard and grill. He rarely got off his phone the entire time.

"I need to lose ten pounds," Kendra said. We were in her office eating our lunches. It occurred to me that Kendra was, in fact, at least ten pounds thinner than she had been that past winter. Since she'd gotten with Greg, she barely ate anymore. I had lived in the city long enough to understand that WASPy finance guys often liked stick-thin pretty blond girls. Kendra was none of those things, and it seemed to me that if that's what Greg wanted, he would have gone out and found himself that. I didn't understand Kendra's spontaneous obsession with changing.

"I just don't want to be thirty and single," she said to me when I asked her about it. "I mean, do you?"

Having Tobias in the atmosphere since I was barely nineteen meant I didn't think about being single. I knew, as long as he was on this earth, I wouldn't be, not really.

"Have you guys talked about getting married?" Kendra pushed on.

I looked down at my wilted greens. We hadn't. We talked about the future. We wanted to travel. Sometimes we fantasized about a kid—his hair, my sense of balance. It was always hypothetical.

"We're just enjoying where we are now," I said to Kendra. "We're not in any rush."

But the truth was, of course, *I* had been thinking about it—alone, in secret. Tobias coming back felt significant in a way I wanted to make real. Marriage didn't mean any promise of togetherness. I had learned that lesson young from my mother. But even so, I wanted it to be official. I wanted to stand up and make known those commitments to each other, in front of the people who mattered. There was paperwork and a community, a shared life. I wanted that tether to him. And Jessica had been on me lately. *You've basically been together for five years*, she'd say. *What's his plan?*

I didn't know, and I didn't feel I should ask. I wanted to believe he'd make it, that we'd someday have money to do the things our friends were starting to do, but he'd left his job to be with me. I wasn't going to start in on him now.

"You're so confident," Kendra said. She was dabbing at her eyes with some smoky charcoal pencil she now carried around. "I wish we had that in common."

I shrugged. I didn't feel confident. Most of the time I felt completely unsure. But I loved him, and he loved me. That had to be enough.

That night, a week after the night at Matty's apartment, Tobias and I cooked pasta and ate in bed. It was dripping hot outside and the air conditioner only worked in the bedroom. The rest of the apartment hung at a cool ninety degrees. I never knew if having the windows open or closed made it worse.

"Where do you see yourself in five years?" I asked Tobias.

He burst out laughing. His fork went flying and hit the pillow. A smattering of tomato sauce looked like a mini crime scene.

"Here." I dipped a dishcloth in my water glass and handed it to him. "I'm serious."

"With you," he said, sensing what this was about.

"I know," I said. "And work?"

Tobias scrubbed at the pillow. "I don't know. This gig is fine. Why are we playing this game?"

I took a breath. I plucked up the courage. "Because Kendra asked me today if we're getting married, and I didn't know what to tell her."

Tobias didn't stop scrubbing. "Tell her it's none of her business."

"But it's mine," I said. "Jessica asks me, too. Shouldn't we at least talk about it?"

Tobias stopped and looked at me. "Do you want to?" he asked.

"Yes."

He seemed to consider this for a moment. A change of plans, a subway reroute, a rainstorm in the forecast for a summer picnic.

"That's good to know," he said.

"What's that supposed to mean?"

Tobias sighed. "It means what it means. It's good to know. I didn't know marriage was so important to you, and now I do."

"I didn't say it was so important. I just said we should talk about it. That's what couples do when they've been together as long as we have."

Tobias set his plate down on the nightstand. "By all means, tell me what other couples do. We should take notes! How are we even surviving on our own?"

"That's not what I meant."

"No, that's exactly what you meant. You're never okay with us being *us*. You always need to make sure we're falling in line." He was getting angry. The vein on his forehead twitched when he was worked up.

"Is it so terrible for me to want what other people have? Jessica and Sumir—"

"Because they're the picture of happiness?"

Tobias liked Sumir, but they were nothing alike, and I knew, although he'd never said it, that as Jessica had judgments about our life, Tobias's lack of steady income, our nuclear ways, Tobias had his feelings about theirs. Being stuck, being normalized—those were the things that kept him up at night.

"What's so wrong with them?" I was yelling now. I could feel my heartbeat in my ears. The pasta shifted dangerously in my lap.

"That's really the life you want? To move to Connecticut? You don't even see her anymore. They'll never travel. They'll be stuck in that house and then a bigger one and then a bigger one . . ."

"Yeah, well, at least they'll be together." And there it was—the thing that was always underneath the surface of our fights. *You could leave again.*

"Do you trust me?" Tobias asked. The energy was out of his voice.

"Yes," I said. I exhaled all the air I had been holding. "Of course I do."

"Do you need me to marry you to prove I love you?"

"No," I said. I hung my head and looked at the mess of pasta on my plate. It seemed so stupid now that we were downshifting. I had been whipped into a frenzy by Kendra—why?

"You know there are no guarantees in life, and that I can't promise you anything for certain, just like you can't promise me anything for certain."

"But I can," I said. "I can promise you." I took his hand. "I love you so much."

His green eyes looked into mine. He tucked some hair behind my ear. "I love you, too," he said. "It's gross how much. You know that. There's nothing I wouldn't do for you to be happy."

"Five," I said.

He raised an eyebrow at me. "Hot," he said.

I moved his hand to my chest.

"I was talking about outside, but this, too." He gave my boob a light squeeze.

"Neck." He kissed me there. "Promises."

"Really?" My voice had an edge to it, he could tell.

He tilted my face up with his hand. "Sabby, if what you really want is to get married, we can go to the courthouse right now. Anytime. I want you to be happy."

I felt my chest pull. I knew he did. I knew he meant it.

"Love," I said.

"Love last," he said. "First sex."

He pitched me back onto the bed. We didn't talk about marriage for another year.

9:58 P.M.

O F COURSE WE WERE HAPPY," Tobias says. He's still holding my hand. "But sometimes it felt like we left too much up to fate."

"Interesting," Conrad says. He's leaning forward, his elbows on the table. Audrey swats them off.

"Sabby had this idea that we were fated to be together."

I try to pull my hand away. It feels like he's exposing me in public here tonight. I don't like it. I thought we had a contract to stay in that place together.

"Stop," he says, holding my palm steady. "It's true. You were always pissed I didn't remember you from *Ashes and Snow*."

He's not wrong, strictly speaking. Although *pissed* isn't the right word. *Sad* is probably closer to it.

"She had this sense it was just supposed to work, and you weren't supposed to have to work for it," Jessica says. "Like their love story was so epic the day-to-day didn't matter. But that's what relationships are. They're the day-to-day."

"I'm right here," I tell her. I pull my hand out of Tobias's so I can more properly face Jessica. "Can you please stop talking about me as if I'm a child in the other room?"

Jessica rolls her eyes. "I didn't say that. I just . . ."

"What?" I snap at her. "You didn't want me to be with him. Just admit it. You act like you loved him."

"I went with you!" Jessica says. She's gesturing wildly now. "I practically *pushed* you. I was the one who found that photography club. I was the one who drove you to UCLA."

Tobias is looking at me curiously. "You never told me how you got that photo."

"Of course I did. After *Ashes and Snow* I didn't even know your name. I went to UCLA. I found the photography club. You weren't there, but I bought that photo."

"No," Tobias says. "You never told me that." He looks concerned, stressed. Flushed like he's just come in from running.

"See this, right here? This is what I mean!" Jessica says. "You both always thought it was coincidence, but it wasn't. You needed everything to seem like magic. You couldn't accept that you were both human."

We found each other again, against all odds. In New York City! We were magic.

"I didn't need magic," Tobias says, mostly to me. He still looks alarmed.

"Where did you think she got the photograph?" Audrey interjects. "Surely . . ."

"You knew," Robert says. "You just didn't want to admit it to yourself, because of the responsibility it would mean, because of what you'd owe her."

Robert's tone has changed. There is something almost paternal in it. It makes us all stop and look at him.

"No," I say. "Come on." Because if I'm going to defend one of them, it's going to be Tobias.

Tobias exhales. "He's right," he says. "I think so, anyway." He runs his hands over his face. I feel my body tighten next to him. "Sometimes I was scared of letting you down," he says. "You thought so highly of me. I wasn't always that person."

"I *saw* you," I say. "I saw us. I saw this whole future. . . ."

Tobias looks at Robert. The two of them exchange a glance, and for the first time tonight I take them in like this, sitting next to each other. They look nothing alike. Tobias with his big head of curls and bright green eyes, my father with his near-balding head, patched skin, and sunken chest. But there's a nervous quality to them both. They're on high alert. I remember a still image, like a snapshot, of my father pacing in the kitchen, his fingers nipping at one another. An uncomfortable thought presents itself. I push it back down.

"Fine," I say. "You were human. I was wrong about you. It was my fault."

"That's not what I said," Tobias says. "It wasn't your fault."

I hold my arms out. "Well, if it wasn't my fault and it wasn't your fault, then what?"

Silence falls over the table. I hear Audrey clear her throat. Finally, Conrad leans forward.

"Then we order dessert," he says. Audrey shakes her head at him. "What?" he says. "I need something sweet."

We each busy ourselves with our menus, the heat of the last few minutes hanging in the air between us. The words all swim together until I can't make them out. He did love me the way I needed to be loved. Being with him was all that ever mattered. And if we can't figure this out, if we can't go back, he's going to be lost to me forever. It doesn't feel like we're getting any closer. In fact, it feels like we're getting farther away.

"Soufflés?" Conrad asks, and the group starts talking about ice cream and sorbet and peach cobbler, and I sit back and wonder what would happen if I just got up and left. If I walked out of the restaurant and home. They'd disappear. My father. Audrey. Conrad and Jessica, too. But then Tobias would be gone for good, and I can't have that, not with so much still left between us.

FIFTEEN

AFTER THAT SUMMER, AFTER THAT NIGHT of pasta and marriage talk, we settled into a routine for the fall and winter. Work, home, cook, sex (sometimes), sleep. It wasn't the summer of fun and freedom anymore, it was life—and we weren't always completely compatible.

We began to fight more than I'd like to admit. That West Village apartment wasn't always a love shack, and it wasn't always big enough for both of us; in fact, it rarely was. When we had lived with Rubiah, and even Jessica before her, there had been a buffer. Now it was just the two of us knocking up against each other. Sometimes we crashed.

But it was part of *us*, I reasoned. It was what made us spark, what made us different from Jessica and Sumir, from me and Paul. We could love and fight in equal measure, and that contact, I told myself, was good. It meant we were passionate. It meant we cared.

Tobias had developed a few habits in the two years he was gone, and so had I. My relationship with Paul had been, if not particularly charged, then definitely full of ease. We never fought, mostly because there wasn't much to fight about. The relationship was suspended in warm water—impact-proof. We traded off on delivery menus, museums, and movies. We were like teammates passing a baton back and forth without any of the running, stress, shouting, or inevitable wins.

I remember once going over to Paul's after work and finding him on his computer. I had a key after month two, which had more to do with efficiency than romance or commitment. "What are you doing?" I asked him.

He looked up at me and handed me a glass of wine. He always had one ready when I came over. "Making a spreadsheet," he said.

He turned the computer around and showed me. "See? Areas of the city, then museums, restaurants, and special events." He ran his finger along the top of the screen. "So we don't have to check *Time Out* so much. I'm condensing everything for our Saturdays. And some weeknight things as well."

I took a sip of wine. "That's genius." It was exactly the sort of thing I would have done, and I liked that I didn't have to, that he already was. That I hadn't even thought of it.

He smiled. "Thanks." He handed me our stack of delivery menus. "Here, your turn."

Our similarities in lifestyle made it so that we didn't come up against each other all that often. The only fights, if you could even call them that, we got into were never about our relationship. They were about the background of an actor we'd seen in a play, whether or not he'd been on *That '70s Show* (which of course was solved with a quick Google). *The Washington Post* versus *The New York Times*. The best place for a weekend away. Him: Fire Island. Me: Berkshires. We cleaned the kitchen before we went to sleep and both set our alarms for 7:10.

Whatever Paul and I were, Tobias and I were the exact opposite. We were all contact. Dirty dishes and piles of laundry and empty toothpaste tubes and broken radiators. We were sweat and spit and heat and thump-thump-thumping. We were so real it drove us crazy.

The first novel I'd edited on my own was coming out in March, and I invited Jessica and Sumir, David and Kendra to come to the launch. It was a middle-grade novel titled *The Sky for a Day*, and it was about a little boy who discovers he has the ability to fly. I was proud of it and the author—a fifty-year-old debut writer named Tawnya Demarco. I couldn't wait to share it with everyone, especially Tobias. I wanted him to see that while he was gone I had been working on important things, too.

We all gathered at McNally on a Tuesday at six. It was raining outside, and I feared Jessica might bail out, but she showed up first, and then Sumir twenty minutes later. David came with a new boyfriend, Asher.

David hugged me. "Congratulations, beautiful! I can't wait to see Tobias," he said. "It has been actual years."

We had plans to go to dinner after, a cozy pizza place around the corner called Rubirosa that was impossible to get into. I'd made reservations the month before.

"He's excited to see you!" I said.

Tobias wasn't social. He was personable and engaging, and when he met you he was genuinely interested, but he never wanted us to make plans. In the beginning, before California, he had made an effort with my friends, but it seemed his inherent tendency toward isolation had gotten worse as time went on. *Why go out?* he'd ask me. *Everything I want is right here.*

Tawnya was nervous. I poured her half a glass of cheap red our publicist had supplied and told her she'd be great. She was doing a short reading and then a Q and A. I went to the mic and told people to take their seats. Jessica, Sumir, David, and Asher sat in the second row. Jessica gave me the thumbs-up. Where was Tobias?

"Thank you all so much for coming," I said. "I'm so proud to introduce this woman and her beautiful book . . ."

I spoke about falling in love with the book on my first read and how talented and commited Tawnya was. When I sat down the room broke into applause to welcome her, but Tobias wasn't there. All through her reading I kept glancing toward the back, expecting him to show, but he didn't.

Once I'd congratulated Tawnya and set her up signing books, I checked my phone. I had a missed call from him and a text. *So sorry baby I'm caught at work. Tell your friends hi and knock em dead. Love you.*

I just kept staring at his words. *Your friends.* Not ours. Not David, Jessica, and Sumir.

"You almost ready?" Jessica asked. She had a signed copy of the book tucked under her arm. "Where's Tobias? Is he meeting us there?"

I stuck on a smile. "He's stuck at work. It'll just be us."

I saw Jessica send a sideways glance at Sumir. I knew what she was thinking: *My husband can make it to your event, why can't your boyfriend?*

We went to dinner and everyone toasted the book, but I was

distracted. I wanted him to be there, I wanted him to share this. But more than that, I wanted him to understand how important this was to me. I wanted him to exist in the world with me, the real one—the one made up of my job and friends and life. Not just the one in our apartment.

When I got home he was watching TV on the couch.

"How did it go?" he asked. He shut it off as soon as I walked in. "Tell me everything." He handed me a bouquet of sunflowers. It was March; I didn't know how he'd found them.

"Good," I said. "I missed you."

"I'm sorry," he said. "I got caught up taking photos. The sunset was incredible tonight. Did you see it?"

"I thought you were at work," I said.

"I was working," he said.

I didn't feel like fighting. I went to put the sunflowers in water. He hadn't.

That night I just kept thinking about Jessica's look to Sumir, about how David had shown up with a man he was just dating.

❧

Tobias had taken up Transcendental Meditation in L.A. He liked to wake up in the morning, sit in a chair, and meditate for twenty minutes, as was protocol. But our apartment was tiny, and with two of us, there wasn't room for both silence and speed in the morning. I had to be at the office at nine, which meant I had to leave at eight-thirty. I tried to walk to work, as my gym time was woefully lacking, but most days I ended up taking the subway. I would stumble around

Tobias, opening drawers, trying to find tights and matching shoes, as he sat there with his eyes closed in pursuit of tuning out the world.

"Can't you do that the night before?" he'd ask.

"Can't you do that once I leave?" I'd fire back. Tobias had a flexible schedule. This job was turning out to be more mind-numbing gigs than Digicam, and as fall turned to winter and winter turned to spring even the commercial work waned and waned. He was still employed, but they assigned other people to cover the ad work probably, I thought but kept to myself, because Tobias wasn't very good at hiding his disdain for it. His boss started traveling more and bringing another assistant on shoots. I didn't bring it up to Tobias because I knew it was a sensitive subject, but more than once I wondered why he didn't look for another gig. These jobs weren't easy to come by, I knew that, and I knew it's what he would say if I brought it up to him. He was becoming increasingly deliquent in rent, something he paid me, because my name, for logistical reasons, was on the lease. Sometimes he forgot entirely, and when I'd remind him of it, weeks later, he'd be incredibly apologetic. "I'm so sorry," he'd say. "I forgot. I'll have it next week."

"He needs to step up," Jessica told me on a rare lunch we had in the fall. We were eating at a chain Greek place we both liked. "You want to have kids. Who is going to provide?"

"*Provide?*" I said. "Do we even use that word anymore?"

"I do." Jessica looked right at me. "You earn like four cents an hour." She paused. "How is everything else?" she asked.

"Good," I said. I shifted under her gaze.

"Do you want Sumir to talk to him? You know he loves Tobias; we both do. I just think it's time you guys face facts."

"And what facts would those be?" I asked.

"That you're going to need to grow up one of these days."

I thought about Jessica in college—lighting incense in our kitchen and charging crystals on our bedroom windowsill. What would she think about herself now? Would she be disappointed? Angry? Would she feel betrayed?

That was so much of it—I didn't want to betray Tobias and me. We were meant to be epic. We were meant to hover above the normalcy. I didn't blame Jessica for not seeing that, but I also didn't know how to explain it to her—the same rules didn't apply to us.

On one particular day in late April I was running late. Random House was having a big launch meeting at nine A.M., a quarterly meeting where editors present their upcoming titles to sales and marketing. I had a PowerPoint to finish for my boss and was supposed to get in at eight A.M. but had overslept.

I was rattling around the bedroom, yanking open drawers, trying to find my brown corduroy pants.

"Can you please keep it down?" Tobias asked from his meditative perch.

"No," I said. "I can't. I'm late for work. *My* job actually has prescribed hours." I knew as soon as I said it that it was the wrong move, but it was too late. It was already out there.

"Wow," Tobias said, opening his eyes. "Way to get that out there."

"I just mean your shoot isn't until one," I said. "You can meditate once I'm gone."

"This is my apartment, too," Tobias said. "Even if you never fucking act like it."

He left the bedroom. I remember watching his foot at the door. He was still in his sweatpants.

I didn't act like this was my place. It was ours. We had moved in together. But I had taken on this role of being the responsible one. Sometimes I even felt like a parent. I cleaned the dishes when they piled up, and I noticed when the milk was bad or empty. I called the super when the radiator stopped working and bought the lightbulbs when the kitchen went dark.

I came home that night and found him in the kitchen. His sweatpants were on; I didn't know if he'd been to work that day or not. But he was making lasagna, my favorite. I smelled the garlic and bubbling tomato sauce, and when I dropped my bag down and went into the kitchen he held out a wooden spoon for me to taste.

"It's perfect," I said. We didn't talk about the morning, but I knew that this was his way of apologizing, of making it right.

"More salt?"

I shook my head. I kissed him with tomato sauce lips. "Perfect."

I made a salad with arugula and onions and some pine nuts I found in our cabinet. Tobias was always buying food supplies I didn't think we could afford, but this time I didn't care. I was grateful for all of it, for the way the food was bringing us back together. We ate on the living room floor because we didn't have a table, and because there was something romantic about being young and broke and in love. And when you're young and broke and in love you eat lasagna on the floor. Although it didn't escape me that there was a difference between being broke at twenty-two and at twenty-eight.

I didn't mention the job because I knew we agreed—this wasn't what Tobias wanted either. I knew that, for him, it was the worst kind of settling. It wasn't creative, and it wasn't sexy. It didn't even pay well. What I didn't know, and what terrified me, was whether he blamed me. If the opportunities he could have had if he'd stayed in L.A. weighed on him, and if I was on the other side of that scale.

We had sex in the one club chair, which had traveled with us from the old apartment, and left the dishes in the sink. The next evening, when I got home from work, they were cleaned and put away.

10:10 P.M.

WE ORDER DESSERT. FOUR SOUFFLÉS. Jessica gets ice cream. Audrey and Robert order cappuccinos, and Tobias and I get espressos.

"You know what I think we need?" Conrad says. "A time-out."

"We don't have time," I say. "This can't possibly go past midnight." One night only. It's only poetically fair.

"That's two hours from now," Robert says, as if to say that's plenty.

"What are you suggesting?" Audrey asks Conrad. "A conversation on politics would hardly be a break."

"In this climate, no." Conrad shakes his head. "Although I do often wonder what those of your generation who are gone would think about the world now."

"Nothing good," Audrey says. "It's quite appalling."

"Indeed," Conrad says.

"Everything moves so fast now," Robert says. "It's impossible to keep up."

"What's it like?" Conrad asks. I expect him to take out his pocket pad, but he doesn't.

"Good," Robert says. "Not bad."

"No," Audrey says. "Not bad. The getting dead I could have done without, but the rest of it is . . . kind of lovely. You needn't fear it."

"No!" Robert says, as if this point is obvious. "There is no need to fear it."

Tobias is quiet. Conrad looks to him. "And for you?"

"Different," Audrey says. Her tone has changed. It's more empathetic.

Tobias nods. "Yeah."

"What do you mean?" I ask. My heart starts racing. Is Tobias somewhere he doesn't want to be? Is he in pain?

"More in-between," he says. He smiles at me, the kind of smile I know takes effort, the one he puts on for my benefit and mine alone.

"What does that mean?" I ask.

He leans over and tucks my hair behind my ear, even though none of it has fallen in my face. "You want to know what I remember?" he asks me.

"What?" I say. I feel close to crying. He's so near, and his words are so tender.

"Those days with you at the beach."

"Where are you?" I ask him again. But then I think of something. If he's not there, if he's not wherever Audrey and Robert are, then there really is a chance for us. I really can get him back. He's not as far away as they are.

"My early years with the children," Audrey says, from across the table. "If we're doing a highlights reel."

Tobias blinks back from me, and I have the urge to leap across the table and throttle Audrey. We were so close, a whisper from something, before she spoke.

"And Paris," she says, taking us further and further away from the moment before. "I miss it."

"Of course," Conrad says. He taps her wrist gently. "Robert?"

"My highlight?" he asks.

Conrad nods. I hear Jessica next to me sigh audibly. "My first year of sobriety. The birth of each of my children."

"Are they like Sabrina?" Audrey asks.

Robert smiles. "I'd like to say yes. I mentioned Daisy likes to sing. She's in a conservatory for directing, writing, and performing. I know her mother worries about her ability to provide for herself with such a creative career, but I think she'll be okay."

"Is she talented?" Audrey asks.

"Very," he says. "And stubborn—like you, I think?" Robert looks at me and then blinks a few times rapidly. "Alex is much more reserved. She grew up quickly; she was always an old soul, and she married quite young, actually. I was still there for that."

"You walked her down the aisle," I say.

"I did."

"Nice for her." I don't want to be, but still I'm bitter. I feel the emotion in my throat like the remnants of cough syrup—sticky and dense. And since we're almost out of time, I ask him.

"You got better and they got you," I say. "And all I had was a drunk father who left before I could even remember why."

Robert exhales. "I can never make right what happened, but I'd like you to know them," he says. "They always wanted to meet you."

I know this. I have a letter from Alex sitting in a box at home. I never opened it, even though it's been more than ten years. It felt like a betrayal to my mom, somehow, to be in touch with her. To want more than what she gave me. So I didn't.

But she's not here tonight. Only Robert is.

"Alex is a dentist, you said?" Conrad asks.

I see Robert's eyes light up. "She's training to be an orthodontist. She's very bright and does quite well. Oliver . . ." He pats his coat pocket and then seems to remember himself.

"It's true what they say," Audrey reacts. "You can't take it with you."

Conrad chuckles. "I'm still going to try."

Jessica squints at Conrad. "You mean you're not . . ."

"Dead?" Conrad nearly screams it. "Most certainly not! I am very much alive. Whatever gave you that idea?"

Jessica shrugs. "You just give off the impression."

"Of being dead?" Conrad asks. "How flattering."

"No, she means wisdom," Audrey says. "About life, which makes sense. It is best suited for the living."

"I know I can't ask anything of you," Robert says to me. "But if I could, I'd like you to look them up and meet them. I think it might help."

"Help?"

"Sabby," Tobias says. "You know what he means."

"I don't think it would," I say.

"It might," Jessica says. "You don't know."

I look at her, because out of everyone she should understand. Her mom had another family. Jessica has three younger brothers she helped raise. Her mother was a teenager when she had her and a grown-up when she had them. And then she died and left Jessica in charge of it all.

"I love my brothers, you know that," she says, reading me. "They made a lot of it worth it. And those girls miss him. Just like you do."

"I don't even know him," I say.

I look at Robert. He's sitting upright, his face drawn, but his eyes are wide open. I can register the pain my comment has caused, but I see something else there, too. He looks hopeful.

"I have a lot of regrets," Robert says. "I should have left Jeanette more money. She's okay, but I worry about her. I wish the girls were a little older. I didn't get to see Daisy graduate. She needs a father now. She fights with her mother a lot. I wish I had met my grandson."

"Do I have to sit and listen to this?" I say.

"Yes," Robert says. And it's the first time I've heard him speak with authority all night. He looks taller, and younger, too. "I have a lot of regrets, Sabrina. About my whole family. But I am here with you. Tonight I am here with you."

Happiness is a choice.

"He's right," Tobias says. "You can be angry, you can hate us, but we're here for you. All of us."

It's so much, it's too much. Tobias in purgatory and Robert with his regrets and me, mourning both of them, still. "Alex wrote me a letter," I say. "I never opened it. I was just too . . ." I look to Robert. "I guess I didn't want it to be that easy."

Robert looks down onto the table. He holds his fist to his mouth and clears his throat.

Our coffees arrive then.

"Oh, how delightful, foam art! I completely missed foam art," Audrey exclaims. She clasps her hands together and peers down at her cup. It doesn't even appear performative, although she is, after all, an actress.

"*You* are the delight," Conrad says to her.

Audrey blushes.

"And I don't hate you," I say just to Tobias. But I know the table can hear. "I miss you." I look up just an inch when I say it and catch Robert's eye.

SIXTEEN

OUR LAST SUMMER, TOBIAS GOT AN assignment in the Hamptons photographing the new Montauk Inn. I took a vacation day and went out to the beach with him. It had been a rough winter and a rougher spring. His unhappiness with his job and our opposing schedules were taking their toll. I knew we needed the time together. He knew, too, and he arranged the whole thing. He asked for a bungalow right on the beach (which the shoot paid for), he asked me to get off work, and he picked up my favorite wine and brought it out with him.

Tobias borrowed Matty's car (he had one of his own now) and drove out east on Thursday. I followed on Friday and met him at the Montauk train station. I took the LIRR out after work, a ride I hadn't done since our first year in New York, when Sumir's boss at the law firm had lent him his house for the weekend and Jessica and I had piled into the train with Two Buck Chuck, Scattergories, and bags of popcorn. We were only out there for a long weekend, but it felt like a month.

When I saw him standing on the platform, holding a single sunflower, I knew instantly we were okay. It was him. Tobias. *My* Tobias. Not the grumpy, downtrodden guy who sometimes inhabited our home, but the boy I fell in love with on the Santa Monica Pier all those years ago.

I leapt into his arms. He picked me up and spun me around. I could smell the salt water on him. "We really should stick to beaches," he said.

That night we cooked lobster and dipped it in butter sauce on the bungalow's deck. I had brought in four bottles of white wine from the city in addition to his red, and we drank two of them snuggled in a chair together. I was wearing his sweatshirt—an old one from UCLA that smelled like him. I remember thinking that this was the heaven I wanted to be in—this, right here. The two of us and butter and the sunset—making everything fluid and hazy and golden.

"Why do we fight?" he asked me. "We don't need to. It's stupid." He nuzzled his face in the crook of my neck. I felt his nose graze my collarbone.

"I know," I said. "It is stupid. I just want you to be happy, and sometimes I feel like you're not."

"I am," he said.

"Now." I sat up and put my hands on his chest. "But sometimes I feel like you blame me for the work stuff. Like if you had stayed in California you'd be shooting for *Vanity Fair* by now."

"That's crazy," he said, but it wasn't, I could tell. He was trying to bury his tone.

"It's not." I turned his face to mine. I looked into his eyes. "You came back for me, but it's not enough if you don't really want to be here. I love you, but it doesn't mean anything if you're not happy."

Tobias shifted me in his lap. He brought his face close to mine so that I couldn't see his features, just the smooth square of skin. "I've blamed the situation," he said. His voice was low and hoarse—near a whisper. "But I don't want to anymore."

I felt his heartbeat on my chest, the warmth of his breath on my chin. "Okay," I said.

"It's not fair, I know. But I need you to forgive me."

"Tobias."

"Please?" he asked. Although it wasn't a question.

"Of course," I said.

I kissed him and he wrapped his arms around me. He carried me into the bedroom. It was all white and blue with little accents of sea-foam green.

I didn't think much more about it. I didn't think what it meant, that he had admitted it to me. I just thought about the fact that he wanted to let it go. He had, in a moment, decided our future was more important than our past. It was as simple as that.

"Let's just stay here," he said to me. We were in bed, naked, our limbs entwined like tree roots.

"We could fish for sustenance," I said.

"I'd learn the ways of the hunter."

I laughed. The idea of Tobias hunting anything was comical. He hadn't so much as had red meat in six months—a fact he thought I hadn't noticed, but had. He'd left a copy of *The Omnivore's Dilemma* lying around the house. He hadn't mentioned it, but slowly he'd started to transition his diet. He stopped ordering burgers—not that they were a staple. But he'd started buying vegan imitation meat and roasting portobello mushrooms as a protein.

"I'd gather. Weeds and nuts and seeds. We could build a home of bamboo."

Tobias raised his eyebrow at me. "A tree fort?"

"Cool in the summer, warm in the winter," I said.

"Sounds perfect," he said. He moved his hands on me underneath the blanket. "Just the two of us."

I didn't think, but I should have, about his comment. How all our fantasies—his and mine, ours together—revolved around us being alone, somewhere other people, the world with all its politics and societal demands, couldn't touch us. We were the best when we were separate, uninterrupted. The beach, our apartment, a bedroom with the windows closed. Our problem wasn't us together, it was us in the world—a world that demanded we reconcile its reality with our romance. *If only*, I remember thinking, although I wasn't sure what.

10:17 P.M.

"I S THERE SOMETHING YOU WANT TO SAY?" I ask Jessica. She has
been shifting and sighing in her chair for minutes—a sure sign
she has an opinion on something.

"You don't care what I think," Jessica says. "So why are you even
asking?"

"That's not true," Tobias says over me. "I care."

Jessica exhales and rolls her eyes at him. But it's friendly. I have
a flash of them playing gin rummy on the living room floor together,
and Tobias throwing his hand to let her win.

Robert busies himself with his cappuccino. From across the table,
Conrad and Audrey lean in.

I open my mouth to say something, to counteract her, to tell her
I want to know, of course I do, but I think about what she's said. I
didn't care, not when Tobias and I were together. I felt pressure

172

and then annoyance—mixed with the pain of the fact that she had broken this contract between us. Lifelong friends. Ride-or-dies. I wanted to be where she was, but I also knew Tobias wasn't ready for that kind of real life. Maybe I resented her for having it.

"I do, too," I tell her.

Jessica sighs. She tucks some hair behind her ear. "You both thought you loved the other one more."

If I were honest, I did feel that way. I tracked him down. I bought that photo. I held on to us like we were some kind of guiding star. And then later, I was the one who walked on eggshells when things were rocky, who made concessions and tiptoed around my bedroom and paid our rent and whispered.

"Maybe that's true," Tobias says, which comes as a surprise. I didn't think he'd cop to the imbalance in our relationship in such broad terms.

"I loved you more," I say. "I don't blame you—I chose that role—but it was me. Gardener, remember?" I try for a smile.

Tobias runs a hand over his face. His neck muscles tighten. It's the first time all night I register his annoyance—maybe even anger. It wafts off him like cologne.

"The fact that you think that means it's not true," Tobias says. "You didn't love me more. If anything, I loved you more. I gave up my job to come back for you. You never fully let me in. You always had an escape plan."

The familiar tilt in his voice makes my stomach turn over. It's the same tone he used during those mismatched mornings. Next to me, Jessica nods, which makes my irritation match his.

"See?" Jessica says. "You both started to be resentful of all the things you thought you'd given up for the other one, and that resentment took up all the space—it pushed everything good out. It was hard to watch."

Tobias shakes his head. "I wanted you to be happy so badly, Sabby. It just felt impossible sometimes."

"It felt impossible to me, too," I say. I feel stubborn, defiant—this is not what was supposed to be happening now. This is not how we get back.

"So you loved each other too much," Robert says. "Is that possible? If you love, is there even such a thing as a yardstick?"

I think about that. I would never think my love for Tobias had boundaries, limitation, a quantified amount. It was endless. And I didn't believe I had a choice in it. We'd found each other again—in New York City!—and against all odds. Our story couldn't end any other way than us together—even if it made both of us miserable sometimes.

"The person who believes they love more believes they give more," Jessica says. Her tone takes on a wilting, guru quality reminiscent of our early years. "And that can lead to resentment."

"No shit," Conrad says.

We all turn to him, surprised. Conrad hasn't sworn once all night.

"These things aren't perfect," Conrad says. "When I met my wife I was down on my luck. I'd just been fired from the first university I'd ever worked at. I had no money. I wasn't sure I'd ever teach again."

"What happened?" Audrey asks. Her tone is breathless and her hand flutters to his forearm.

"Budget cuts to the department. I was a relatively new hire, and so I was the first to go. It wasn't personal, but I took it hard. Twenty-seven years old, you understand."

Audrey nods.

"She worked at the local library in Santa Rosa, and I'd go there to work and scan for job openings. This was before the Internet, of course. We were confined to pen and paper."

Conrad chuckles to himself. "We fell in love over Faulkner and Yeats. She'd bring me new books to read whenever she saw me. Eventually, she asked if she could cook me dinner. I must have appeared a poor sight."

"Where were you living?" Jessica asks.

"Old tenement housing," Conrad says. "A bed and a washbasin. I was too embarrassed to bring her there, so I suggested a picnic in the park."

"How darling," Audrey says. Her eyes are big and wide.

"She showed up with a basket of cheeses and this strudel she'd made. Still the best thing I've ever tasted. She took me in after that. She had an apartment on the outskirts of the city, and I lived there for two years, working odd jobs, before another university position came up. She paid our bills, those two years, with her librarian salary. I could never repay her."

Conrad gazes off, and I realize the thing that's been staring me in the face all night.

"What happened to her?" I ask softly.

Conrad looks back at me sharply. "Early-onset Alzheimer's," he says. "About five years back now."

Robert jumps in. "I'm so sorry," he says. "That must have been very painful."

"She didn't want to live too long with it. When she was diagnosed, she made me promise."

"We didn't know," Audrey says. "Oh, goodness. I feel terribly." She pats his arm where her hand has lingered. It doesn't now.

"How old was she?" Jessica asks.

"Sixty-four," Conrad says. "Too young."

"Much too young," Jessica agrees.

A lump has formed in my throat, so ripe and full that I'm afraid if I breathe too deeply all will come out are sobs. This man. This man who has sat here all night, listened and given, offered and been patient, has lost someone, too. And the woven web of us, of all of us—of the people who aren't here but should be—makes my hands tremble.

We're here with you, Tobias had said. But I understand now. The significance. How big of a sacrifice they're all making.

"We both loved more," Conrad says. "We just took it in turns."

I look to Tobias. *Love is a state of mind.*

"You must miss her terribly," I say to Conrad.

He nods. And then he does something peculiar. He winks at me. "And yet," he says, right across the table, so that it feels like it's only the two of us among the dinner crowd. "The beat goes on."

SEVENTEEN

THE FIRST NIGHT AT THE BEACH opened into morning, and still in a haze of love and wine and sex we woke up early and drove into Amagansett in Matty's car. We found a spot easily—it was early enough that the streets were nearly vacant. The only people out and awake were parents with their young children, presumably letting the other partner sleep in. Tricycles tottled down the road, training wheels bumping behind. A couple in jogging outfits passed by us, talking.

We got coffees and muffins at Jack's and then walked down to the beach. It was early, maybe seven A.M., and I was still wearing Tobias's sweatshirt. Besides a few early-morning runners and two women practicing yoga, the beach was ours. The salt air was cold and the coffee was warm and the sand was wet. I cuffed my jeans at the ankles and we decided to stroll.

"I'm so glad we did this," I said. "It's heaven out here."

The beach was foggy and gray—it felt as cozy as a fireplace and red wine in winter. I grew up in California, and still there is nothing quite like an East Coast beach to me. I had the feeling, walking along the shore, that if I sent a bottle out into the sea it would keep going until it reached its destination. From the shore everything looked wide and open and calm—which was, in that moment, how I felt about us. The details of life that had begun to weigh on us didn't exist out here. There were no alarm clocks or opposing schedules or underwhelming jobs.

"I'm glad we came out, too," Tobias said. He pulled me in and planted a kiss on my cheek.

"We should come back in the winter. I bet no one's here."

"Shh," Tobias said. "Let's focus on now."

He took my hand. His fingers were warm from holding his coffee and I curled mine around his. We walked like that, barely talking, for upward of half an hour. The ocean was meditative—the crash of waves felt energizing and lulling all at once.

When Tobias dropped to his knee, I thought he had fallen.

I offered my hand to help him up. My gaze was out on the ocean. It wasn't until I heard him say my name that I turned and realized he was kneeling.

He was wearing that smile—golden and wide with just a hint of mischief. "Hey, Sabby. I wanted to ask you something."

"No," I said, although it was the exact opposite of what I felt. All of it—every cell in my body—was lit up with *yes*.

"I love you. It's as simple and as complicated as that. There's no one else in the world for me. You're it."

"You're kidding," I said. "Stop. Come on." I couldn't believe it. It felt surreal—like we were just in a watercolor and at any moment might be washed away.

"I'm not." Tobias looked up at me, and I saw the boy I had met all those years ago on a very different beach by an entirely different ocean. "Sabrina, will you marry me?"

The sea crashed next to us, and I remember thinking I wanted to scream my answer. I wanted to compete with the wild force of the water. But I also remembered our conversation a year ago and Tobias's resistance.

"Are you sure?" I said, trying, in a moment, to ground us. I didn't want this to be because of me. I wanted it to be because of him. I wanted him to want it.

Tobias smiled. It was close to a laugh. "I'm asking you to marry me and you're asking if I'm sure."

"Yes," I said.

"Well, now, that's tricky. Yes, you're asking if I'm sure or—"

"Yes," I said again, cutting him off.

He pulled me down into the sand and kissed me. There was no ring; I didn't even notice.

We went back to our bungalow and had chilled champagne and, when it started to rain, took the comforter from the bed onto the love seat and watched the movie we had that first time—*Roman Holiday*. Tobias downloaded it on his computer and hooked it up to the TV with some kind of jumper cables.

Tobias had made reservations at the Grill—a fancy East Hampton establishment—but we ended up canceling. We ate complimentary sour-cream-and-onion potato chips and drank the red that Tobias had brought out instead.

There were no frantic calls to parents or Instagram posts. All that mattered on that East Coast beach was us and the promise we'd just made to each other. *Forever.*

10:28 P.M.

SOMETHING IS HAPPENING BETWEEN Conrad and Audrey. We're still waiting on dessert, but they've turned toward each other and for the last three minutes have not been engaging with the rest of the table. He refills her water glass and then, in a flourish, retrieves her dropped napkin from the floor. The rest of us have left our side conversations and are watching them like act three of a movie.

"This can't end well," Jessica whispers to me.

"How come?" I ask.

Jessica looks at me like I'm nuts. "She's dead, remember?"

I think about Conrad's wife, how he's been alone these last few years, what he probably wouldn't give to be at dinner with her. And yet his words: *The beat goes on.*

Conrad leans over and whispers something in Audrey's ear, and she laughs, a hand placed delicately on her heart.

"Excuse me," Jessica says to them. "What's so funny?"

Audrey seems caught, like she's momentarily forgotten where she is. "Oh," she says. "Oh, I'm sorry. Conrad was just regaling me with an anecdote about the theater."

"I'm sure we'd like to hear, too," Jessica says. She's ribbing them, but Tobias and I are probably the only ones who notice.

"Nonsense, we're old-timers here. Just having a look back," Conrad says.

"I swear to it," Audrey says. "I don't think I'd be able to live today. These cell phones—everyone buried in them."

"Tell me about it," Robert says. "The girls won't put them down. I used to hate them, but I know my wife appreciates them now. When she's not with them she gets to do—" He holds his hand in front of his face as if he's speaking to it.

"FaceTime?" Tobias offers.

"Right. FaceTime with the baby."

"How do you know that?" I ask. "You were gone before he was born."

"I check in," Robert says, almost sheepishly. "On you, too."

I look at Tobias.

"Yes," he says.

I open my eyes and close them again. Audrey's shoulder is now touching Conrad's. Neither of them is moving.

"Just with people you love?"

"Sure," Audrey says. "Although as you go on . . . you do it less. It becomes necessary to move on, even there."

She holds my gaze and I look away. "Do you wish you were still here?" I ask her. "Would you want to be?"

Audrey glances at Conrad. "That's a hard question to answer," she says. "I'd be very old."

"Would you have wanted more time?" I ask.

"I could have done more work with UNICEF," she says. "I loved my later years with them; I would have liked to do more. And the children, of course."

I can't help but think that doesn't really answer the question, and I can tell Audrey knows, too.

"You don't miss it, if that's what you're asking," she says. "Life is very difficult. This is not."

"She's right," Robert says. "It's like the sweetest Sunday, really."

If I had known, if I had prepared, if Tobias weren't sitting next to me with time running through an hourglass, I'd have questions. I'd want to know what happens when you die, whether you pass through a tunnel, whether there's a light. I'd like to know if you can hang out with people, if you see everyone you lost again—and what the deal with reincarnation is—but there is only so much we can accomplish in one dinner, and the priorities of this one have long been set.

"Fascinating," Conrad says. He pats her arm, and she blushes.

"You'll see," she whispers, in that signature breathless voice that made her so famous. A hush falls over the table. Even Tobias is looking at her as if drugged.

"And you?" Conrad asks Tobias. "You said it was different."

"I said it, actually," Audrey says.

"But it's true?" Conrad asks.

"Yes," Tobias says. "It is."

"Why?"

Tobias looks at me. "I think I'm still between," he says. "I'm hopeful this dinner might sort some of that out."

"Is that common?" Conrad asks.

"I don't know," Tobias says. "I don't think so."

Again, I feel that spark of hope. He's not gone. Not yet. In fact, his admission makes me feel closer than ever to bringing him back.

Next to me, Jessica doesn't say anything. She's looking down into her tea, and I see, in fact, that she's crying.

"Jess," I say. "What's wrong?"

"You think she watches Douglas?" she asks me. "She didn't . . ." She breaks off, and I am reminded, of course, of her mother. Of the cancer that came to claim her. Of the absence of her. At Jessica's graduation. Wedding. The birth of her child. What wouldn't she do to have one dinner with her? To get one night to tell her everything that happened and all the ways it was unfair? To sit in her presence and touch and gaze and mourn?

"Yes," I say. "Of course."

It's this realization—that this dinner, whatever it may not be, is a stroke of luck, of fate, of fortune—that makes me turn to Robert.

"I tried to find you," I tell him. His head snaps from Audrey to me faster than a falling water droplet. "I found out you were in California. I even got so far as your house, but I couldn't bring myself to knock on the door."

"When?" Robert asks.

"I was sixteen, maybe," I say. "I borrowed Mom's car, and she called me when I was sitting in the driveway. I don't remember about what. When I was coming home or what I wanted for dinner. But as soon as I hung up with her, I turned around and left."

Robert hangs his head and nods. "I understand."

"It felt like a betrayal," I say. "I'm sorry, I wish I would have gone inside."

"Your mother?" Conrad asks.

I nod.

"She would want this for you," Audrey says. She leans forward onto her elbows—something she hasn't done all evening. "She might not know it now, but she would. The petty stuff . . ."

"This isn't petty," Jessica says a little defensively. "He left them. Jessica's mother raised her."

"I believe you told us she asked him to leave," Conrad says.

"She didn't have a choice," Jessica fires back.

I have a flash of fierce love for Jessica, and I remember how much she loves my mom. How whenever my mom would send a care package to our apartment it was always for "the girls." And when she would come to town the three of us would go to dinner. She still buys Jessica birthday presents every year. She knew Jessica's mom was gone and took it upon herself to sneak in, however peripherally, wherever she could.

"Of course," Audrey says, still sitting forward. "These things are not mutually exclusive. He did leave. And yet he's here now. And Sabrina's mother would want her to forgive him."

"Oh," Robert says. "I don't—"

"You do," Audrey says. "That's why you're here."

I look at Conrad, who stares straight back at me. "Is she right?" he says.

I think about my father, about Tobias, sitting next to me. About all the ways the men in my life have not lived up to what I needed from them. But I told Tobias I wouldn't stay with him. Wasn't I responsible, too?

I look at Audrey. I see a strength there I've never seen before—not tonight, and not in all my years watching her onscreen. Her features, her voice, her body were always so birdlike, so delicate and complex in nature that the simplicity of power never seemed relevant. But now I see her seated here in all her regal glory, and she is big and bold—she takes up the whole room.

"Of course she's right," I say, still looking at her.

"Forgiveness," Conrad repeats, like it's a stone he's turning over in his hands. "It's more for the bestower than the bestowed."

"First there's something I have to tell you," Robert says. "It might change your tone."

"Go on," Conrad says. "Time is wasting."

"The story I told you? About the baby your mom lost?"

"Yes?"

"The miscarriage wasn't from natural causes. Your mother was in a car accident."

"Oh dear," Conrad says. "Poor woman."

Jessica winces next to me. I don't have to hear the rest to know what's coming.

"I was driving," Robert says. He looks at me, and his eyes are full of pain. I think, briefly, of the promise of afterlife—freedom from suffering.

"I was drunk. We had gone to dinner in New Hope, and I was driving us back. I'd had too much wine. Your mother had asked to drive, but I told her I was fine—she was pregnant, you see. I didn't want to tax her." Robert holds his fist to his mouth. "We were going to name her Isabella."

"Beautiful name," Audrey says.

Robert gives her a small, sad smile.

"I did this," Robert says. "I don't expect your forgiveness. I don't deserve it."

I think of Jessica's mom, Conrad's wife. This strange opportunity I've been given.

"You do," I say. In my lap, my hands shake. "We both do."

EIGHTEEN

"TOBIAS *PROPOSED*?!" I WAS ON THE phone with Jessica, on the train back into the city. Tobias was staying in Montauk for another five days to finish up the shoot. She'd screamed when I told her, and asked me to clarify three times. "Tell me everything."

I was trying to think of the last time Jessica had seen Tobias. I didn't know. Maybe in the winter, at their holiday party? She and Sumir had thrown one at their newly renovated house, and we'd gone. She'd paraded us around their home, calling out the need for improvements, as their friends, people named Grace and Steve and Jill, trailed behind. I had no idea where she'd met them. The grocery store? Where does one meet Connecticut friends before one has kids?

"And this," Jessica had said, "will be Sumir's office. Once I clear some clothes out of here." We had arrived at a small room down the hall from the master bedroom suite. It had only one tiny window and a fan overhead.

"An office, huh?" Jill had said, and giggled. Jessica had stuck her hands on her hips and shook her head in a girlish way, a way meant for sorority girls and wives on television shows in the fifties. *A baby*, I remember thinking.

And one of the friends—let's say it was Grace—asked about us. "Are you married?"

"No," Jessica had answered for me, with a little too much heat. "They're against marriage."

"We are?" Tobias had said. He'd draped his arm over my shoulder and pulled me to his side.

"We're definitely anti-divorce," I had said.

"Right!" Tobias had exclaimed. "That's the one."

Jessica had rolled her eyes. "You're children," she had said. I didn't understand then how much she had meant by that, but now, on the phone, I could hear her glee and something else, too—relief. I was finally doing the thing she wanted me to do. Maybe, just maybe, we'd end up back on the same side.

"We were out at the beach," I told her. "We went for a walk in the morning. It was early, like seven A.M. He just got down on one knee and asked me to marry him."

A man in a baseball hat next to me took out his earbud and gave me a pointed look before putting it back in. I lowered my voice.

"What did he *say*?" Jessica pressed. "I need you to be specific here."

"He said he loves me and asked if I'd marry him," I said. "It was simple."

"Oh my god," Jessica repeated, more than once. "Did you say yes?"

From anyone else it would have been a throwaway question—a joke, even. But from Jessica, I knew it wasn't, at least not entirely. I paused. I could feel the curl of anger in my stomach. It was as if she had asked, *Will you really go through with it?* or *Are you finally admitting you're normal, you're like everyone else?*

"Of course I said yes." I tried to keep my voice level.

There was a pause on the other end of the line. Then: "I'm happy for you. When can we start planning?"

Tobias and I hadn't spoken about the wedding. We'd spent the weekend in bed, talking about where we wanted to travel to and what we wanted to do with the apartment—China, get curtains for the bedroom. We hadn't mentioned summer or winter, a church or outside. It hadn't even occurred to me to bring it up.

"I don't know," I said. "It just happened."

"Okay, well, text me a pic of the ring immediately."

Strike two. There was no ring. Tobias had said the proposal had been spontaneous. "But of course I've been thinking about it," he said. "I want to spend my life with you, you know that. This isn't a whim." But nevertheless he hadn't purchased a ring. He didn't have the cash right then anyway.

"We still have to pick it up," I lied. It wasn't the first time I had lied to Jessica. But it was maybe the first time I had lied to her about Tobias—and that lie felt bigger. It was a lie about our future, Tobias's and mine. With this lie—about our wedding, a marriage I did, it turns out, long for—it felt like I'd never stop. That our entire future would be half truths and edits. All my elation from the weekend settled down into my stomach and turned to dread. It jumped around in there like bad oysters.

I arrived at home and there was a note on the door from the super. Someone was coming to check the drain system tomorrow at three—could I be there?

I dropped my bag by the door and flopped onto our chair—the one that had migrated over from the Chelsea apartment. I thought about calling my mom, but she'd want the same details Jessica did, and I didn't have them. The balloon of happiness I'd experienced at the beach with Tobias had been punctured by the call with Jessica—I didn't want to relive that.

I called Tobias.

"Hey," he said. "Is everything okay? I can't talk."

I could hear the sounds of production around him. "Of course," I said. "Yeah."

"Sabby, what's wrong?"

"Do you think it's bad that we didn't talk about the wedding once this weekend?"

He paused. I could hear the air through his mouth—in and out, in and out. "Are you serious?"

"No," I said. "Yes. Maybe."

"Look, I gotta go." He sounded annoyed. No, he sounded disappointed. Like I had turned out to be just like all the rest of them—all giggling and tulle and baby's breath and pink ribbon. It made my stomach turn, too.

"All right, I'm sorry, have fun."

"We okay?" he asked me.

"Great," I said.

He hung up.

My unease about my call with Jessica grew to anger. As much as I tried to pretend, often unsuccessfully, that Jessica's disapproval of my life didn't bother me, it did. I wanted her to understand me the way she used to. I wanted her to make fun of Beth and Jill, not be them. I wanted her to roll her eyes when someone suggested Sumir's office could be a baby's room—because babies, really? Didn't we shudder at the idea? Didn't we laugh and say we'd never be able to give up booze and sleep? That was us, right?

It's like all the things she had believed, the deep truths she assigned to the universe, were now girlish fancies, silly dreams she was too mature to entertain. And the crazy thing was we weren't even thirty yet. This was New York. A baby before thirty was a cause for concern, not celebration. No one gets married at twenty-five. She was the one who had chosen a different path and had to move to another state just so there'd be people who understood her life choices. This wasn't my fault; it was hers.

I started to get worked up in the chair in our tiny apartment. She judged my life so harshly all the time. I was engaged, and it wasn't good enough. *I* was never good enough.

I called her back then. I wanted to yell at her that I didn't want to do this anymore. That I no longer knew what I had done so wrong, that I was sick of this pretend friendship. That she wasn't the person I'd signed up to love. That as she felt I wouldn't grow up with her— that I wouldn't . . . what? Move to the suburbs and have a baby next door?—I was sad and angry that she'd left, that she'd so readily and easily and joyfully given up on everything we had been—but her voice mail picked up. *Hi, it's Jessica Bedi. Please leave me a message and I'll get back to you as soon as I can. Thanks! Bye!*

I hung up. Jessica had even changed her name. She used to be Jessica Kirk; now she was Jessica Bedi. I matched her judgment with my own until I felt bigger, better. All she wanted to talk about was babies and throw pillows, and whether the shade of eggshell she had chosen for her dining room (she had a dining room!) was too blue. She wasn't even pregnant yet. I explained to myself that she had sold out and was jealous that I was still here, in the city. I ignored the fact that being a New Yorker had never been Jessica's dream. She had always wanted Sumir like I had always wanted Tobias. Whose fault was it that our realities were so incompatible now?

I remember she called me back an hour later. I picked up. She sounded tired, like she had just woken up. "Sorry I missed you," she said. "What's up?"

"Nothing," I said. "I dialed you by accident."

10:35 P.M.

Y OU'VE BARELY SAID ANYTHING," Jessica says to Tobias. I have felt her anxiety building. Since I sat down, really, but particularly after Robert's confession, her tears about her mother. The table had been in relative silence for the last few minutes in eager anticipation of our desserts, which are still not here.

"I haven't?"

Jessica shakes her head. "No, you haven't. You keep reacting to everyone else. I still don't know what you really think about all of us."

Conrad raises his eyebrow at me. "You're a tough critic, Jessica," he says.

"Understatement," Tobias says, but he's smiling.

"Well," Audrey says. "Maybe she's right, Tobias. What do you think about all of this?"

"It's strange."

"Obviously," Jessica says, impatient.

"I feel sad," he says. "Sad that Sabby was in pain, that I couldn't or didn't do anything about it. That I died. That wasn't great."

He looks up at me, and I see his right eyebrow is raised, as if he's asking for a smile. I give him one.

"You are the great love of my life," he says. He puts a hand on my face. His fingertips feel like relief.

"This isn't what I meant," Jessica says.

"Jess, stop," I say.

"No, I won't. He's dead, remember?"

Something cold blooms in my veins. "Yes," I say. I feel a chill and hug my sweater closer. "And I'm trying to fix that."

"I want Tobias to be alive as much as the next guy," Jessica says, gesturing idly toward Conrad.

"Thanks," Tobias tells her. "I think?"

"But," she says, holding up her hand. "I think it's a disservice to pretend like everything was always perfect with you guys. It wasn't. There was so much that didn't work. You knew it, too. That's why you wouldn't go to L.A. with him."

"That's not true," I say. "I had a job, remember? I had a life . . ."

"Oh, come on! It wasn't because you were afraid of him cheating on you or your father leaving or any of those bullshit reasons you've given. You weren't sure he was right for you."

Tobias looks to me, but Jessica keeps talking. "I'm sorry, Sabby, but if we're going to do this, we should do it right. There isn't just your side to this story."

"That's not true," I say.

"It is," Jessica says. "You knew he was an artist. You worried about financial stability. You saw him prioritize photography over everything else. Just admit it."

"Stop," Tobias says. He throws his hands in the air. It's the most animated I've seen him all night. "Sabby knew what she meant to me."

"Did she?" Jessica asks. "Because I'm sitting here, ten years later, and I still don't know for sure." Jessica looks back to me. "You wanted what people want. You wanted to get married. You wanted to know you could pay the rent. You wanted someone who showed up. That wasn't a crime. It still isn't."

I look to Tobias. I feel ashamed all of a sudden—exposed. Like this conversation should be happening in private. Not in front of Robert and Conrad and Audrey Hepburn.

"Is that true?" Tobias asks.

"Sometimes," I say, because it's all I can say, barely above a whisper. "I wasn't sure we'd ever get there together."

Tobias looks devastated. It makes me want to weep.

"I need you to know you were always more than enough for me," he says. He swallows. "Now. Tonight."

"It doesn't have to be tonight," I say. "I . . ."

"How delusional are you?" Jessica asks. She raises her voice until she's practically screaming. A few lingering diners even look over. "You're not getting him back! You can't fix it, and you know that, and I can't sit by and let you delude yourself anymore. Take responsibility or don't. But when tonight is over you'll be alone again."

Her words tear through me like teeth. I feel like I've had the wind knocked out of me.

"Jessica," Tobias cuts in. "I think that's enough."

Jessica looks at Tobias. I swear I think she might leap over me and pummel him.

"I'm sorry," Tobias continues. "I never apologized to you. After L.A. I'm sure it wasn't easy having to pick up the pieces."

"That's such a convenient narrative," Jessica says. Her tone is bitter. "The sad young artist who needs to go off and find himself, and the woman who cries herself to sleep at night missing him. You're not characters in a novel. You're human. And neither of you will just fucking admit it."

"You're an artist? I thought you were a photographer," Conrad says, interrupting the tension.

"It's a category!" Jessica snaps. She's getting even more worked up.

Tobias puts his hand up to his forehead and holds it there. "I don't know what you want us to say."

"Something!" Jessica says. "Anything. You heard Robert." She gestures to him with her head. "We only get this one night. Do you want to go back over every detail, or do you want to try and help Sabby move on?"

"No," I say. "Don't help me move on." She's leading us off course. I have to right the ship.

It's now that our dessert arrives. The waiter appears with a tray and starts setting things down. Soufflés and the ice cream and a complimentary sorbet. He asks if we need anything else, and when no one answers Audrey politely waves him off.

My words are still hanging there. I feel Jessica, tense, next to me. All other eyes are on Tobias.

He shifts toward me, and I think he's going to take my hand again—I *want* him to take my hand again—but instead he kisses me. He puts one hand firmly on the side of my face, right up against my ear, and his lips on mine. They're cool—like he's just taken a sip of ice water. But soon the sensation gives way to a folding so big it feels like collapse. It's like I'm being sucked through a vortex to a place that is *him*. He's not *there*; it *is* him. And then it's us. Alone together in some suspended place. And it's then that I realize the collapsing isn't space at all but time. Here, now, he's still alive; we're still together. There is no separation. There is no before or after. There's just us on the beach in Santa Monica, us in our apartment, us playing Scrabble with Matty, cooking dinner with Jessica. Memories piled high on top of one another, and the moment stretched so big it covers them all.

NINETEEN

A MONTH LATER WE GOT A ring. It was a Sunday afternoon in late September, and we were uptown. It was quiet. The weather was still nice, and on the Upper East Side people were taking advantage of the extra warm weekends out East. It felt like we had all of Park Avenue to ourselves—as if that was in some way desirable. We had just come from the Guggenheim. There had been a retrospective on Edward Hopper that Tobias wanted to see, and afterward we decided to stroll. We may have had lunch at Serafina or picked up bagels at Murray's, but for right then we were just walking. It was a bright, cloudless afternoon, just bordering on skin-burning but not quite there. There was still movement on the street and we were both wearing hats. Invincible.

Our hands were intertwined and I remember looking down at them. Pure skin. No metal or even plastic. We hadn't talked about the wedding at all in the last month. In fact, with the exception of a few key friends and family—Kendra at work, my mom, who miraculously asked nothing; I had the sneaking suspicion Jessica had gotten to her first—we didn't talk about the engagement at all. It was starting to feel as if it had never happened.

"I think we need a ring," I said. Tobias was looking in the direction of a French bulldog that had become untethered from its owner. I could tell he hadn't heard me.

"Tobias," I said. He spun his head to look at me. "We're engaged. We should get a ring."

I wasn't sure how he would take it. He had been so irritated on the phone when I had brought it up weeks ago that I hadn't wanted to again. But I was beginning to feel like if I didn't mention it, no one would, and we'd forget and the engagement would never have happened.

"Okay," he said. "What do you want?"

I swung our hands, still interlaced, around me. I pulled myself into him and kissed him on the cheek. "I don't know. I just know I want something."

I hadn't really thought about it. I wasn't one of those girls who dreamed about the big diamond ring. Even if we could have afforded it, which we couldn't, that wouldn't have been for me. I thought maybe a colored stone—amethyst or ruby. Something deep in color and ancient-looking.

"Come on," Tobias said, tugging me forward now. "I know a place we can check out."

We walked down to Seventy-first Street and then made a left. Between First and Second Avenues was this tiny antiques shop. Tobias had never taken me, but he'd mentioned it before as somewhere he sometimes went. He had sold an old leather briefcase there when I'd first known him in New York—back when he needed a quick hundred bucks. I guess he still did; I just didn't think he pawned things anymore.

The shop was down a flight of stairs in an old brownstone building on a modest block. The owner, a woman named Ingrid who appeared to be in her seventies, let us in when we buzzed. She kissed Tobias twice—once on each cheek. She seemed happy to see him but not surprised.

"Handsome," she said, holding him at arm's length. "With a little bit of the devil."

Tobias smiled. "Ingrid, this is Sabrina. Sabrina, Ingrid." He leaned in close to her like he was revealing a secret. "Sabrina is my fiancée."

Ingrid's eyes went wide, and she clasped her hands together, turning to me. I was hanging back, letting them have a moment, but Ingrid extended her hand out to me and I stepped toward.

"You," she said to me, patting my hand, "are a charmed woman."

I shook my head. I could feel Tobias's hand find my waist. "She is," he said. "I'm very lucky." He spun his thumb up under my shirt. "And now we need a ring."

This was the most we'd talked about the engagement since he'd proposed. I felt dizzy, delighted. Like everything I needed was right there in that little shop on Seventy-first Street. Ingrid included.

"Let's look," she said. She took my hand in hers and with the other she took her glasses from where they dangled around her neck and put them on. The closer I got, the more I could smell her—the headiest, sweetest vanilla fragrance I'd ever encountered.

Ingrid peered down at my hand. "Beautiful," she said. "Very delicate extensions." She picked up a finger and wiggled it around like she was testing it, like she was trying to find a loose piece. "Follow me."

There wasn't a single other customer in the store as Ingrid took us into a second room. Here were racks of coats—most of them dried-out fur. I cleared my throat in an attempt to stifle a cough.

"Here we are." Ingrid went behind a glass case, took some keys out of her pocket, and opened it. She reached inside and took out a velvet tray on which were set rows of rings. "Pick one," she said.

At first glance, they all looked antique—Victorian, even—but as I peered closer I started to see all kinds of different periods and styles. There were some diamonds, although small. There was a large array of bands, too. Pavé and sapphire and one with tiny threads of white and yellow gold.

"They're beautiful," I said.

"Many happy marriages," Ingrid told me. "I try and see if a marriage is happy, and if it is? I buy. No divorces."

I didn't stop to think about the impossibility of that—if people were happy, why were they getting rid of their rings? Had they all died? And if so, how could you be sure?

Tobias laughed. His hand was now on my shoulder and he started kneading there. I suddenly wished this was all being recorded—that I'd be able to see the replay tonight, next year, a decade from now.

"What about that one?" I pointed to a ring with three small emeralds in yellow gold.

"No, no," Ingrid said. She shook her head. "You need something more traditional."

"Oh," I said. "I'm not really . . ." I looked up at Tobias. "I'm not that traditional."

"No?" she asked. She peered at me for a moment. "Here. Try this."

Ingrid handed me a white gold ring with a small diamond solitaire surrounded by yellow amethysts. To this day, it's one of the most beautiful things I've ever seen. I couldn't believe I hadn't noticed it right away.

"It's gorgeous," I said. "But I think it's a little too much." What I meant was expensive. The ring looked like it would cost our rent for the year.

"Just put it on," she said.

Ingrid didn't seem like a woman to disobey, and so I did as she said. I slid the ring over my finger. It glistened on my ring finger, proud. I shifted my hand gently in the light, watching it sparkle.

"Let me see." This from Tobias.

I spun around and shook my hand like I was in a rap video. "Bling, no?" It was ridiculous, I knew. But it was still fun.

"That's serious," he said.

"I know."

"How much?" he asked Ingrid.

"Normally, five thousand," she said. "But for you, three."

That was triple what we'd be able to pay. I immediately took it off. "That's too much," I said. "But it's beautiful. Is there anything else?"

"Sure, sure," Ingrid said. "But nothing like that one. I call her Rose."

Tobias had gone quiet behind me. I went in search of his hand. "Hey," I said, tugging him closer. "What do you like?"

"I like that one," he said. He looked determined. "The one you had on. We'll buy it."

"Tobias," I said. I moved toward him and lowered my voice, trying to give us the illusion of privacy. "It's way too much, come on."

"Isn't the man supposed to buy the ring?" he asked me. But it wasn't a question. It wasn't fun anymore. It was tinged with aggression.

"Yes, but baby, I don't need that one. Let's just pick something else, okay?"

I rifled through the rings. There was a sweet one with small chips of diamonds and amethysts in an intricate gold pattern. "How much is this one?" I asked Ingrid.

"Seven hundred," she said. "It's very sweet."

I slipped it on. It fit perfectly. "What do you think?" I asked Tobias.

He barely looked down at my hand. "It's fine," he said.

"Tobias," I said. "Fine isn't good enough. Do you want to keep looking?"

He shook his head. "Sorry, it's really nice." He picked up my hand gingerly. "It looks great on you." He gave me a small smile I knew was taking a lot of effort.

"I love it," I said. I meant it, too. It wasn't the first ring, but it felt good on my hand. I knew I wanted to leave it there.

"We'll take it," Tobias said.

I snuggled into him. He put his arm around me. We were trying at the moment. I wanted to recapture some of that playfulness I had felt when we first walked in.

"It's a wise choice," Ingrid said. "It looks lovely on you." She didn't seem any more or less pleased that we were going with the ring that was five times cheaper, and I felt a rush of affection for her.

We followed Ingrid back past the coatracks and into the main room. She stood behind the register and I watched Tobias take out his wallet. Seven hundred dollars was still a lot of money, money he didn't have, and I knew it, but something told me not to offer to chip in. Tobias put a credit card down.

We hugged Ingrid good-bye and climbed the stairs to the street. It was markedly cooler than when we'd gone down. "I love it," I told him. I looked down at my hand—the ring was twinkling in the last rays of summer sunshine. "And I love you."

He pulled me toward him. "You sure you're happy?" he said.

I wanted him to add *with the ring*, but he didn't.

"Of course," I said. "The happiest. I get to marry you."

"Yeah," he said. He nodded a few times.

I reached up and took his head in my hands. "This is all I need," I said. "It's all I'll ever need."

He hugged me then so tightly I almost couldn't breathe. We clung to each other on that late afternoon as if we saw what was coming.

10:42 P.M.

WHEN TOBIAS'S LIPS FINALLY LEAVE MINE it takes me a second to remember where we are. Dinner. The list. I touch my fingers to my lips and blink back out at the table. Audrey and Conrad are looking at us. Robert is busying himself with his soufflé, and Jessica has her arms crossed next to me.

"I'm sure that fixed everything," she deadpans.

"I miss being kissed like that," Audrey says. Her voice is low and breathy, and then she startles up and looks at Conrad. I imagine, under the table, they've brushed legs.

Tobias is looking at me like he's trying to gauge my reaction, but all I can think is that I want to know how he feels, what he's thinking. I want to take his hand and run outside and take him home.

"Sorry," Tobias says to me. "I didn't mean to . . ." Tobias looks to Jessica. "Did you want us to get married?"

"Of course," she says, but her words are unconvincing. "I wanted you guys to be happy. This isn't about me."

"It kind of is, though," Tobias says. "You won't stop talking, and you're here."

"Yeah, but I'm not kissing her. Plus, I'm alive." Her face sneaks a smile, and Tobias notices.

"Jess," he says. "Conrad is very much alive, as are you, and Sabrina."

Jessica rolls her eyes, but the smile is still there.

"We used to have fun together," he says. He scoots his chair so he's facing me, talking to her. "Remember the night we drew all over Sabby in Magic Marker and put toothpaste on her feet?"

"She deserved it," Jessica says. "She made us miss *Book of Mormon*."

"It was my birthday," I say.

"Yeah, twenty-fourth. You should have been able to handle your booze better." Tobias needles me with his elbow, and Jessica laughs.

"You were *so* pissed," she says. "You didn't speak to either of us all day."

"Correction," I say. "I was puking all day."

"Still," Tobias says. "That was us."

Jessica leans back and nods. "Yeah. It was. But that was a long time ago."

I feel the air charged around me. Like I'm the space between the positive and negative ions. The dense collection of yes and no trying to come together and apart, together and apart.

"Maybe you shouldn't have taken me back," Tobias says. He's leaning forward with his hands clasped over his knees. "After L.A. Maybe you should have moved on then, stayed with Paul, I don't know."

I think of saying no to that buzzer, of not letting him up and back into my life. But it was never a viable option. When Tobias came back, there was no alternative.

"I never asked you to stay," I say. Not even to him, to the whole table. "I couldn't come to L.A. with you, but I never asked you to stay."

"Why didn't you?" Audrey asks.

"I was too proud. Or too afraid, I guess. That he'd say no. Or he'd say yes and then resent me."

"Would you have, Tobias?" Audrey's voice floats in on the breeze. "Would you have stayed?"

I want him to say no so badly I can practically taste it. It feels ripe in my mouth—a berry about to be plucked.

"I don't know," he says. "Or no. I guess the answer is no. She didn't have to ask; I went. I hated it, but I had to."

"And you came back?" Audrey asks. "Why?"

"Because I couldn't live without her."

The table hangs in silence. No one moves, not even to pick up a wineglass.

I never questioned that Tobias was the one for me, but what if all this missed opportunity, strife, and heartbreak didn't point to the epicness of our relationship but instead its precariousness? Its fragility. Maybe Jessica was right—we hadn't grown up, we hadn't taken responsibility. I somehow believed the universe would do it for us. I believed it tonight, still sitting here. But what if the work had been up to us all along? *Timing is everything*, Jessica told me when he left. And tonight, we are almost out of time entirely.

TWENTY

O NE DAY IN EARLY OCTOBER, Tobias came home to tell me he wanted to strike out on his own. The time had come. Things at the new gig had gotten worse and worse. Not only was he miserable, but he felt like he had taken ten steps backward since the course he'd been on in L.A.

I knew he wanted to return to photographing what he loved, and I knew it was just a matter of time before he'd want to pursue another job or begin to build his solo résumé. The fact that it was at this juncture, when he was dead broke, when we were barely making rent and had just gotten engaged, didn't seem to be troubling him. He was a ball of energy as soon as he walked in the door.

"I've been thinking about it for a while," he said, coming to sit with me on the couch. "But today it just hit me—why wait? I want to be able to focus on my own work."

"Wow," I said. "Okay." Living with someone who didn't like his job, who I now knew felt resentful, wasn't fun. I wanted him to be happy, and I wanted him to finally have the career I knew he wanted. But I also wanted to sleep indoors, and eat, and have a wedding. I tried to do the math. "Tell me what you're thinking."

I could feel his excitement, and I went to get us something to drink. I pulled a bottle of expensive champagne Matty had bought us as a housewarming gift when we moved in that we'd been saving. I brought it out with two glasses. If we had to talk about this, we'd talk about it with booze.

"I'll give my notice tomorrow, they'll find someone, and I think Lane will probably fill in in the meantime." Lane was another assistant who was part-time. Tobias liked her. "And then, first things first: I need to build a Web site." Tobias was talking with his hands, the way he did when he was really animated. I popped the champagne and poured.

"I'll get Matty to help me on the tech stuff, and then I want to approach the clients I worked with in L.A. I don't expect all of them will say yes, but maybe one or two. . . ."

I handed him a glass. His eyes were shining. I had seen it so rarely those days. On the beach in Montauk, maybe not since. If what he was saying was true, if the work would come, I wanted to get behind him. Maybe this was our problem. His unhappiness with work had leaked over into our personal life. If he started getting happy there, he'd be happy here.

"Cheers," I said. "I think this is a great idea."

"Yeah?" Tobias looked a way he very rarely did: sheepish. "I mean, I'd maybe need you to cover the entire rent for a month. Two, at the most. But then I'll be making way more than I do now, and I'd pay it all back. . . ."

My heart started to speed up in my chest, but I didn't let it show. I put my hand over his. "Baby," I said. "That's fine. We'll make it work." I was little more than scraping by at Random, but I had some savings. My parents had bought bonds when I was born and sold them at my college graduation—the money amounted to about ten thousand dollars and had grown since. I'd use that. It was worth it to see him this happy.

"I love you," he said. He kissed me fiercely. "And I want to start talking about the wedding. We should do it in the spring. Why wait, right?"

My heart seemed to expand out of my body. It grew so big that it encompassed us both. It thumped all around us.

"Spring," I said. "That sounds great."

"Or we could elope." He took my glass out of my hand and set it down. He pulled me into his lap.

"Like Vegas?" I asked. I put my hands on his face. He hadn't shaved in a few days and his chin was all stubble. It tickled my skin as I rubbed back and forth.

"Like city hall," he said. Tobias leaned in to kiss me and then pivoted me around until I was straddling him.

"My mom would freak," I said. I was breathless now. We still had sex often, but it had lost some of the intensity, the connection I used to feel before L.A. And here it was again, blazing between us on the couch.

"Don't forget Jessica," Tobias said, working my neck. "She'd kill you."

"She'd kill *you*," I corrected him.

We looked at each other and burst out laughing.

"Have you shown her the ring?" he asked.

I had. We'd had dinner the week after, and she seemed happy. All she wanted to do was talk about the wedding—where we'd have it, what I'd wear. I let her. I had fallen more and more in love with the ring the more I wore it. I didn't even take it off at night. I loved the small hint of gold, the way it picked up the sun.

"Yes," I said. "She said it was nontraditional. You know Jessica. She just needs to feel like things are her idea."

"Even me?"

"Even you," I said. I kissed him on the cheek. "I've learned some things from our sales and marketing departments," I said. "You should make Twitter and Instagram accounts with your photos, and I'll help you promote them."

He threw his head back in a show of disdain.

"It's important," I said, needling him. "You need to create a presence."

"A presence."

"A presence."

"How do you think I'm doing right now?"

"Decently," I said. I raised my eyebrow at him, and then in one swift motion he picked me up and threw me over his shoulder.

Tobias wasn't much bigger than me—taller, maybe a touch sturdier, although barely since he'd gone vegetarian. He'd lost the muscle mass he'd returned from California with. I teetered on his shoulder as he stood up and wobbled to the bedroom. He clutched my legs tightly as he tossed me on the bed.

"I think this is going to be good," he said. "I can feel it."

I felt, if not convinced, then relieved, alleviated. There was something to focus on now. I felt like we had finally found the thing to solve, and the way to solve it.

10:48 P.M.

W E ARE DEEP INTO DESSERT. Ice cream will only hold its shape for so long.

"I was never one for sweets," Audrey says. "But this is delicious."

She lifts a bite of praline ice cream onto her spoon and feeds it to Conrad, who opens his mouth willingly.

"Divine," he says, licking his lips.

"Incredible soufflé," Robert says. "I used to try and make them, but I never quite got the rise right."

"The trick is not to overwhip the egg whites," Audrey says.

I try to imagine Robert in his kitchen, an apron on, a doting wife chopping up vegetables and two little girls at his feet. If he were a friend, I think, I'd have been happy for him.

"So good," Jessica says, her mouth full of a giant bite of soufflé.

Tobias sips his espresso. He turns to me. "I never regretted coming back," he says. "Sometimes I was upset that the work stuff wasn't turning out the way it had in L.A. But it wasn't your fault, and I should never have made you feel like it was."

"We were getting married," I say.

"We were," he says. It's sad; he's sad.

"I was never sure you really wanted to," I say.

"I did," he says. "When I asked you to marry me, I meant it."

"And after?"

He runs a hand around the side of his neck. "I don't know," he says. "I wanted to be with you, but I wanted a lot of things. I wanted a lot for you, too, if you'll believe that."

"I do," I tell him.

"So you never got married?" Robert asks. "I notice you're not wearing a ring."

He sits up a little straighter and does a flourish with his hands when he asks, like he's fixing some sort of invisible tie.

"No," Tobias says. "We didn't."

"You were close, though," Robert says. His voice is sad. "It must have been so tragic. So much unfinished business."

Tobias hangs his head. "We had set a date, yeah," he says. "But the accident . . ."

"We weren't together, exactly," I say. "We got in a big fight, we hadn't spoken in over a month."

I hear Conrad's fork clatter down on his plate. "You were broken up when he died?"

I feel the tears well up within me. I'm afraid if I speak I'll never be able to stop crying.

"It's okay," Robert says. "It's not even eleven yet." He looks at me, and the hope on his face, the *belief*, splits me right down the middle.

And all at once I know the thing I want to ask him, the question at the heart of the why.

"Would *you* want to change things if you could?" I ask Robert.

I see him weigh it in his mind. His wife, the children. The baking and bruised knees and school drop-offs. The years he filled with them.

"Yes," he says. His voice is scratchy. It catches on the one word. "If I could make things right with you—yes."

"Even if it would change everything?"

Robert clears his throat. "The one thing you can never rationalize is the loss of a child. Everything else. People become paraplegics and they find God. They lose all their money and they say it brought them a deeper level of peace, that they discovered what's really important in life. I have heard people say the worst of things happened for the best. But no one ever says that about losing a child."

Conrad makes a noise at the other end of the table. "Well," he says, but that's all.

I look at Robert. He'd want to go back, if he could. Undo all the life that was lived after. But that doesn't sit well with me. It's all I've wanted since I was a little girl—for him to prioritize me, for him to care, for him to return. But hearing him say it now, I know it wouldn't be right. I'm not the only thing that mattered in his life. There was a family that needed him, too, that deserved to exist, and being my father, now, at this point, would undo all that.

Robert is looking at me with what I can only describe as love. Nervous love, timid love, love that does not know its place or where or how it will be received—but love all the same. And I think that maybe that's enough. For now, at this table, that's enough.

TWENTY-ONE

TOBIAS QUIT HIS JOB THE NEXT WEEK and was out of his office in three days. Not that he'd had much by way of a desk. He came home with a box filled with prints—all of which he'd brought there to begin with.

"Is Lane taking the gig?" I asked him.

"For now," he said in that way that let me know he didn't want to talk further about it. That was Tobias—he could be brash about things. When he made up his mind, that was that.

"That's great," I said. "We should celebrate."

We went to our favorite taco place in Park Slope. We ordered margaritas and gorged on free chips and guacamole. I pulled out a box and set it on the table.

"What's this?" he asked.

"A belated birthday present," I said. His birthday had passed

216

with little fanfare the previous month. He had said he didn't want a present (just a cake, a card, and me with nearly no clothes on), and I'd listened, but I'd been wanting to give him this for a while.

"Sabby," he said. "I told you not to."

"Still."

He opened it. Inside was a pocket watch I had from my father. My mother had given it to me years ago—I couldn't even remember when. It was gold, with a tiny thread of silver around the perimeter.

"I love it," he said. He held it in his hands gently, gingerly.

"It's also a compass," I said. I pointed to the hands.

"In case I get lost." He looked at me, but he wasn't laughing.

"So you can always find your way back," I said.

He took my palm. He kissed my fingertips. When a mariachi band started playing, Tobias held out his hand: "Dance with me?"

The restaurant was small, maybe ten tables total—and it was late, past eleven.

He pulled me in close to him. He was wearing a checkered shirt, one I knew he didn't like, but that I loved and commented on frequently. I knew we were at a cheap taco stand, sharing an entrée and filling up on free chips. I knew we were twenty-nine and maybe too old for this, but in that moment I felt like I was exactly where I needed to be. Tobias was home. It was as simple as that. The rest, I reasoned, would fall into place. Who would worry about money when you had love?

"What are you thinking?" Tobias whispered as he dipped me.

"That we should be in Mexico," I said. "Tulum, maybe Cabo. Or the Caribbean."

"Mmm," Tobias said. "Tell me more."

"You, me, the island breeze. Midnight swims."

"And?"

"Bikinis only."

"Sometimes not even those."

"We could stay at one of those hotels with big canopy beds that just have curtains for doors."

"What about bugs?" Tobias asked.

"This is paradise island, baby," I said. "There are no bugs."

I felt him stiffen in my arms. For a moment I didn't get it, what had happened, and then it hit me. The vacation was fictional. He had thought I meant we should go to Mexico for real, we should take a vacation, and in that one comment I'd expressed to him that I knew we wouldn't. We didn't have the money; of course we wouldn't. But he was still buying into the fantasy. The idea of but maybe, perhaps, what if?

I thought about Paul in that moment. I was ashamed I did. I thought about our trip to Portland. How we'd stayed at the Heathman like it was no big deal, eaten out at nice restaurants, and gone to two concerts, just because. We'd been to San Francisco and London, too. It was all so simple, so seamless, and not for the first time, I missed that—the type of partnership where I didn't feel like the weight of our world was on my shoulders alone.

Two weeks passed, and then two more. Tobias busied himself with setting up the site. He was home all the time, working on his computer. He said he'd just get it up and running and then send out an announcement.

In hindsight, I should have known. Tobias was creative, passionate, extraordinarily talented, but he was missing the link—the thing that hooked that talent to a viable means of income. When he had had the job, and Wolfe before that, there had been structure, order, a system to fall into. He hated the system, but he didn't understand that every business, no matter how creative, needs one.

The photography business was something I had learned piecemeal from my years of living with him. In some ways I was perhaps more equipped to see Tobias's career than he was. Most photographers build their portfolio while still assisting, that much I knew. They began to get jobs from under their bosses—the fallout, so to speak. The gigs that were too far to travel or paid too little or were for a publication that was under the radar. Those jobs lead to more independence, which lead to more opportunity—more contacts. And so it went. But it hadn't for Tobias. Because he had left Wolfe and then worked for someone whose clientele he wasn't interested in. And now, diving completely into his own work, without a system behind him, was risky, particularly for someone like Tobias, who was so susceptible to the ups and downs of his own internal landscape.

In the beginning of his freelance stint he threw himself in full force, and I admit, however naively, to feeling buoyed by his enthusiasm. I knew better, but that knowing felt like a betrayal of Tobias, of his talent and my love for him. I ignored it. I watched as he spent thousands he didn't have—that we needed for rent, for the wedding (we had set a date for the spring at a little church in Park Slope we had passed on a walk and liked)—on new camera equipment. I rationalized that he needed to spend money to make money. I pored over his computer with him, looking at city shots he spent his day taking. They were beautiful. Old men and their grandchildren. Waiters at West Village cafés that made the city look like Paris. Graffiti art. He was going to look for work, he said. He was going to go on desk sides and submit to magazines. He knew all the players. It was just a matter of time before he got his first solo shoot. I believed him.

But as the weeks went on, the plan began to morph. It wasn't about jobs anymore. He didn't want to take another soul-sucking gig, he said. He couldn't do it again. He started taking pictures. Constantly. He missed a dinner with Kendra and her boyfriend. He canceled on a drinks night David and the new guy, Mark, had planned. All he did, all day and night long, was shoot.

"When do you think the Web site will be ready?" I asked him weeks later. I had just come home from work. Penguin and Random House publishing houses had merged not too long before and people were getting laid off left and right. I thought my job was safe, for now—they hadn't quite attacked editorial yet—but it was just a matter of time before they did. I didn't have my own list, at least not an impressive one, and I knew I'd be a hard sell at a competing publisher at the next level. I'd have to start as an assistant editor all over again, and I was nearly ready for a promotion. I was coming to the end of my twenties, too. And I had saved nothing toward the future I wanted. Not money, not time, not even vacation days. I spent everything hoping one day, what? Something magical would happen? Tobias would hit it big? I wasn't even sure what he was doing anymore.

"I don't know," he said. "I think I need more material."

"Really?"

I regretted it as soon as I said it. I could feel the attitude in my voice. He gave me a withering look—like I didn't understand, like I couldn't. I took him in in his sweatpants, and I thought that maybe he was right—I didn't get it. I was someone who supported artists as my profession, but I wasn't one.

"I can help," I added, trying to override, rectify. "I know artists. I help writers all the time. We could put an ad in *The Village Voice*, on

Twitter—you could do some commercial shoots to supplement." I snuck that last part in, but he wasn't even listening.

"I think what I need is an exhibit," he said. "I went up to Queens today and shot a bunch." He pivoted his computer so I could see. There were hundreds of photos of the World's Fair grounds. They were beautiful. I did my usual supportive swoon—"Wow," "I love this one"—but as he clicked through I started to feel less and less generous. Why couldn't he have spent the day photographing a wedding? A bar mitzvah? A dog's birthday party, if it paid? The city was full of people willing to shell out dough for his skills—and I resented that he felt above all that. That I had been at work and he'd been here, thinking of galleries and pictures and not bills.

"What kind of exhibit?" I asked when he was finished.

"You know, a show," he said. "Somewhere I can showcase my work and invite the bigwigs."

"Where?" I asked. I had no idea what he meant by bigwigs. Who said if he had a show any of them would even come? Didn't he already have those contacts anyway? Every next step felt like one to the left. I was beginning to think he didn't even want clients unless they were *Vanity Fair.*

"NYU," he said. "My friend Joseph works in the administrative department at Tisch and said he could put it together." He sounded defiant.

"Tobias," I said. "I can't carry us for much longer."

"I know," he grunted. "That's why I'm working day and night to get this business up and running."

"Great!" I said. "Fine." I took my own computer into my lap. I had an edit I needed to finish for my boss. And I wanted a glass of wine. And to take a bath. And to stop talking about this.

"Sound more like you believe in me," he said under his breath.

I pretended like I hadn't heard him, and he went in the kitchen to make pasta or a sandwich or something and then went into the bedroom and by the time I finished the edit, he was asleep.

I confessed at work the next day to Kendra that I was stressed about money. I'd covered our rent myself for two months, which was half of my life's bond savings. I didn't know if I could go a third.

"You need to lay it out for him," she said over coffee and doughnuts behind closed doors in her office. Kendra had recently been promoted to full-fledged editor, a title I should have had based on how long I'd been there. But I also couldn't deny that the situation with Tobias was affecting my productivity. It was ironic: I needed the job more than ever, but I was performing at half mast. It took me three hours to do something that should have taken one. I was distracted and afraid. Yes, fear was behind it all. I was scared all this would come to a head—and then what?

"It's too much to manage alone," Kendra continued.

I licked some caramel off my finger. "He's so sensitive right now," I said. "He thinks I don't believe in him."

Kendra shook her hair out. She had recently let her bangs grow, and she had this punk-rock look now that worked on her. She was still seeing Greg. "Do you?" she asked. "Believe in him?"

It was a question I should have answered automatically. Of course I believed in him. He was the most talented artist I knew. I had been convinced of his talent since the moment I saw his first snap at the UCLA student exhibit. But I also knew I was biased. I loved him. I was invested in a way that couldn't allow me to be impartial. And I also knew that talent wasn't enough. I had met and read many talented writers over the course of my nearly four years at Random House who never made it through the gates. Some submissions were spectacular, but we couldn't publish everything, and more often than not the savvy writer, the celebrity, the one with the Twitter following and well-curated Instagram presence was the one we signed.

I wanted to believe, the way I had, the way I thought Tobias did, that talent would one day win out—that every great manuscript, photo, painting eventually saw the light. But it got harder and harder to hold on to that vision.

"He's amazingly talented," I told Kendra. That much I was sure of. "I just don't know if it's enough. He thinks the world will fold at his feet, and it just doesn't work that way."

She nodded. "If he were taking concrete steps to build a business it would be one thing," she said. "But I get the feeling he's just out there playing with his camera. It feels like he's taking advantage of you."

The words caused me to plunk down my doughnut. That wasn't Tobias. He would never wittingly use me in a way that didn't benefit us both. But she was right about the fact that I needed to talk to him, be real with him. I couldn't continue on like this—I was hemorrhaging money I didn't have, and I still had hopes of us getting married in the spring. I still wanted a wedding—as trite and unaware as that sounds. I had blinders on. But isn't that part of love? Refusing to see the parts that are so dark, so grim, they would send you running? Or is it that you see them and love anyway?

10:57 P.M.

I HAVE TROUBLE WITH PEOPLE LEAVING," I say. I feel more vulnerable than I did an hour ago—I think, as I look around at us all pulling at our desserts, that we all feel a little bit softer. Time is closing in on us, and I need to be honest about the things in myself that need to be brought to the surface. "You and then Tobias." I nod at Robert.

"And me," Jessica says.

I look at her.

"What?" she says. "I left, too. You think it's my fault. That I should give you more or I abandoned you or you need too much from me, but that's not how I see it," Jessica says.

"How do you see it?" Audrey asks. Her tone is soft, motherly.

"We grew up," she said. "We weren't living together anymore. I got married."

I thought we were done with this when she asked why I'd included her, why she was here, but the pain between Jessica and me runs deep. Probably because the history does, too.

"I know all of that," I say. "But you act like you don't care, like our friendship is a nuisance to you. We only see each other when I suggest it. Sometimes I'm afraid that if I stopped calling you, we would never speak again."

"That's crazy," Jessica says, but she doesn't seem convinced by her own words.

"Is it?"

"I have a baby, okay? My life is different. You never understand *that*."

"It was that way before the baby. You're supposed to be my best friend, but Kendra knows more about what's going on in my life than you do."

Jessica blows some air out of her lips, like a low whistle. "You're incredible," she says. "You're never responsible, right? It's never your fault. People are human, Sabrina! They screw up and they're not perfect and they're selfish and sometimes they're doing the best they can."

Next to me, Tobias pinches the space between his eyes, at the top ridge of his nose.

"Jess," I say.

"Fine," she says. "We'll just sit here and listen as you trash us and nod and apologize. It's your dinner, right?"

Her words hit me like a sucker punch. "I'm sorry if I need too much from you," I say slowly. "But I don't have a family. My mom is three thousand miles away; I live by myself . . ." My voice catches and I hate it, hate that I'm so vulnerable here, hate that I can't seem to just stand up on and move on. Hate that she's right—that it's not her responsibility, of course it's not. She can't fix it, even if I still keep wanting her here. "And I need you sometimes. And I don't always want to have to ask. I don't want to feel like hanging out with me is some kind of chore for you."

"It's not," Jessica says.

"Isn't it? Did you really want to be here tonight? Did you even want to keep up this birthday tradition?"

Jessica looks at me. For the first time I see how tired she looks. There are dark circles under her eyes, and she looks like she hasn't slept in days.

"I wanted you to have a good birthday," she says, which of course is not an answer.

I don't have the answer either, though.

"There are things I have to do now or my life stops working," she says. "I know that's not what you want to hear, it's just true."

"I miss you," I say.

Jessica runs a hand through her hair. "I miss you, too," she says. "I just don't always have the energy to do something about it."

A waiter appears to my side. "Are you finished?" he asks me. He points to the soup of ice cream in front of me.

"Yes," I say.

"You're so hard on me," Jessica says.

"That's exactly how I feel about you," I tell her. "You never agree with anything I do."

"That's not true," Jessica says. "I think you're amazing. Your career, I envy it. I miss having a life like that."

"But you're so happy in Connecticut," I say.

"Am I?" she asks. "You've been to visit me three times in as many years. How would you know?"

It's true, I never make it out there. She never invites me, either, but what came first? My unwillingness to go, or her unwillingness to extend herself?

"I'm sorry," I say. "I really am. I didn't . . ."

"I told you, I don't blame you. This is just what is right now. I don't think there is a ton for us to do about it."

"But what if we just keep drifting apart and never find our way back?"

Jessica sighs. She looks at me, unblinking. "Or what if we do? Can't we believe in that for a change?"

TWENTY-TWO

WHY DON'T YOU BORROW OUR CABIN?" Kendra said to me at work. I was complaining that the city was feeling claustrophobic lately, but in truth it was our apartment. When Tobias wasn't out taking photos he was in the chair editing them. Lately I felt disappointed when I'd come home and find him there—which gave me a sinking feeling every time. "My parents never use it. You could just go up there this weekend and clear your head."

I thought about drinking wine by a fire, locking my phone away, and listening to the wind or trees or whatever nature sounded like— it had been far too long. It was November and the beach was the last time I'd left the city. "That sounds amazing," I said.

"Great, I'll bring the keys tomorrow."

I came home intent on telling Tobias my plan. I thought he'd be happy to have the weekend to himself—and that it would be good for us to spend some time apart.

I walked in the door and the Mambo Kings were playing—salsa music I loved. I could smell the garlic and oil and a mix of spices only Tobias could wield.

I dropped my bag down and tossed my shoes off. His back was to me over the stove, and he immediately turned around, a wide grin on his face.

"My queen," he said. "Welcome to paradise." He put his hands on my waist and guided me to the counter, where a blender full of margaritas sat with two waiting salt-rimmed glasses. "We couldn't get to Mexico, so I brought Mexico to us." He held out a glass to me.

"Yes, please."

He filled mine up and then his and then held his glass out to me. "Viva margaritas," he said.

"To us," I said.

Instead of taking a sip I hooked a hand into the collar of his T-shirt and pulled him in for a kiss.

He set his drink down and lifted me off the counter stool, winding his hands down my back and tugging me in closer.

"I'm cooking," he said against my mouth.

"Not anymore."

It had been almost three weeks since we'd had sex—a record number for us, and one I knew was indicative of something wrong in our relationship. We put a lot of emphasis on sex—or I did. It was good, really good, and when we were in that space together I felt as sure as I ever did about our rightness. When we were out of it I felt fractured, disconnected.

Tobias moved his lips to my cheek. "There are three different kinds of fajitas on that stove," he told me. "Not a chance." He grabbed my butt and then gently nudged me away from him as he went back to the food. I didn't feel rejected, more amused. We were back in the love bubble. I slurped my drink and watched him work.

After we ate, when we were full of fajitas and tequila, I told him the Berkshires plan. Except I didn't tell him I wanted to go alone. I said I wanted us to go together.

"That sounds perfect," he told me.

I was thrilled. It felt like we were on our way to reconnecting, that we had set aside the hostility of the last few months and we were moving beyond it, and I knew this trip would be the reset button we needed. We had done so well in the Hamptons, I wanted us to have a little bit of that back—that fun and spunk and spontaneity that I thought defined our relationship. Home had gotten to be so pressurized—money, jobs, life. I wanted us to go somewhere where all that wasn't hanging over our heads. Where we had more space and clear air. I would have the conversation Kendra and I had rehearsed the week before. In the space and open air, out of the city, Tobias would hear me. We'd figure it out.

That weekend we rented a car and went up to Lenox. Tobias drove and I rolled the window down. It was early November and still fall—crisp and cool, not yet biting—and the leaves hadn't completely fallen. Upstate was a wash of gold and red and orange, and I reached out to put my hand over Tobias's.

He lifted his thumb and rubbed my pinky. As soon as we left Queens behind us, I felt myself exhaling.

Jessica called. I hit ignore.

"You need to get that?" Tobias asked me.

"Nope," I said.

He turned to me and winked.

Kendra's parents' cabin was up a hill that looked over a field of sheep and cows. It was small, one bedroom, one bath, with a little kitchen nook, a fireplace, and a screened-in porch. We had brought up groceries and wine, and I unpacked our provisions while Tobias went about building a fire.

Jessica called again. I missed it. My phone was now tucked into my purse, on silent, as it would stay for the rest of the weekend.

"Do you want a glass of red?" I called to him.

"Open the Nero d'Avola," he said.

I found the wine opener in my bag. Kendra had said the cabin was fully loaded, but I didn't want to take any chances. Forgoing wine for the weekend didn't seem like it would help things.

Tobias went outside to gather wood from a pile by the side of the cabin, and I took the Gruyère and Gouda and grapes I'd bought and put them on a cutting board with some crackers and almonds—the spiced kind from Trader Joe's I knew Tobias loved.

When he came back in I poured two glasses and brought one out to him, balancing the cheese plate on my wrist.

"Here, I got it." He took the cheese board off me and set it on the mantel. I handed him a glass of wine and we settled down in a chair in front of the fireplace as he built the fire.

"Can I help?" I asked, sipping.

He cocked his head at me in that way he did that told me he thought I was crazy but he was charmed by it. Head tilted forty-five degrees to the left, one eye closed. "I don't know, can you?"

"I'll blow on it," I said.

He arched his eyebrows at me. "Oh, you will, will you?"

"Maybe," I said. I took another sip. I let my eyes find his over the glass.

"I think you should stay right there," he said. He stood up and came over to me. He slid his hand onto my thigh and brought his lips up to kiss my cheek.

I pulled him down into the chair with me. We picked up where we'd left off over margaritas. I took his shirt off and ran my hands over his shoulders and down his back. He pulled my sweater over my head and kissed the hollow of my collarbone, the space between my ear and shoulder that drove me crazy.

All we needed was to stay this close. Right up against each other, without any space between us. If we did that, we were good. It was just the world—with all its loud chaos, its demands and people and air—that made us fight, that made us separate, that was driving us apart.

Tobias pulled back and looked at me. He hovered over me, so close I could smell the wine on his lips.

"Did I ever tell you about what happened after we met that day on the train?" he asked me.

He hadn't. We had spent some time talking about the beach— our other beginning—but not that one.

"I got off at the next stop. I walked the rest of the way. I had to call Matty."

"Why?" I asked.

"Because," he said. "I had to tell someone I had met her."

"Who?"

"You." He cupped my chin and brought his lips to brush over my eyelids, my cheekbones, the pad of my lips.

"Stay close to me," I told him.

"Always," he said.

He kissed my ear, then dropped his lips into the dip of my collarbone. I took his hand and led him into the bedroom.

Afterward we played Monopoly and drank two bottles of wine. Tobias made us pesto pasta with grilled chicken. I knew we needed to talk, but we needed this night more. We needed to remember what made us special and different and *together*. I wanted to make love and pasta and hold him in my arms.

We'd talk tomorrow, I reasoned.

Tomorrow.

11:05 P.M.

JESSICA IS HOLDING HER SHIRT OUT, and when I look over at her I see that her top is soaking. She's leaking again and trying to conceal the milk stains.

"Excuse me," she says. She collects her bag from where it sits on the floor and scurries into the bathroom. Watching her scuttle away, holding out her top, hits me straight in the gut. I wish we hadn't fought just now.

"I need some air again," I say. Conrad makes a move to stand, but Audrey puts a hand firmly on his shoulder.

"I'll go," she says.

It's the first time she's stood up tonight, and I notice her crisp black pants end at her ankles and she's wearing a pair of black patent-leather ballet flats. She unhooks her Chanel sweater from where it sits on the back of her chair and loops it over her shoulders.

"After you," she says, gesturing toward the door.

Once we're outside, I want a cigarette. The one from earlier, with Conrad, has reignited my craving. I feel like I want to peel off my skin, roll it up, and burn it when Audrey takes out a pack.

"I don't think this could possibly hurt me now," she says, echoing Conrad earlier. "Would you like one?"

Her whimsical drawl has me nervous. I am alone with Audrey Hepburn.

"Please," I say.

She lifts one, hands it to me, and takes one for herself. She lights mine first, then hers. We both inhale what can only be called excessively. Audrey exhales first; a cloud of smoke envelops her.

"That's better," she says, coughing a bit. "*Non?*"

I smile and follow suit.

"Do you know much about me?" she asks. She wants to know why she's here.

"A little," I say. "Mostly your work." I know more—I know a lot—but it seems a strange thing to say, standing outside with her now. Because the truth is I don't know, not entirely, why I chose to include her. Except that her movies represented something to me. Not just with Tobias, but with my father. One of the only things I had from him besides the watch was an old movie collection: *Charade*, *Breakfast at Tiffany's*, and *Sabrina*.

She nods. "Did you know I was in Holland during World War Two? We thought it would be safe there, you see. We didn't think they'd invade . . ." She trails off and puffs again. "It was a terrible time. Those five years we were barely fed. We used to crush up tulip bulbs and bake with them. I watched friends get carted off. My own brother was shipped off to work in Germany. Had we known what was coming, we may have all shot ourselves."

"I'm so sorry," I say. "I did know, a bit. That must have been horrific. I can't imagine."

"But do you want to know what was worse?" she asks me.

"What could be?"

She shifts her weight, what little there is, delicately from one foot to the other. I'm transfixed—all at once reminded of her riding around Rome, singing in a flat in Paris.

"Decades later I started work with UNICEF, and before I died I traveled to Somalia. Seeing that famine, those children starving . . ." She swallows and I see, even in the lamplight, her eyes filled with tears. "It was worse," she says. "Because I wasn't in it with them. And I couldn't fix it. Two million people starving." She shakes her head and wipes at her eyes. "When you suffer alone it's terrible," she says. "But when you watch other people suffer, innocent people, those that cannot help themselves—it is worse."

She looks at me, and I know what she's saying, what she's trying to convey. "Thank you," I say. "For sharing that with me."

"I was an introvert my whole life," she says. "Quiet, reasoned. Perhaps it's time to open up a bit."

"Can I ask you something?" I say.

She puffs again. "Of course."

"If you could do it all over again, all of it, what would you change?"

Audrey considers this. "I would have gotten married again," she says. "A third time, to Robert. I loved him dearly. If I had to do it again I would."

"That's all?" I ask.

She smiles. "Oh, plenty of things," she says. "But it was a good life. It's best not to dwell."

She turns to me abruptly and I am caught again by the profound beauty of her features here together. She is stunning, radiant. A delicate rose petal—perfect in its symmetry. One that does not ever fade. And she hasn't, has she? I wonder what it must have been like for her at the end, if she ever withered. I can't imagine it.

"I was a romantic," she says. "Until the very end. People always associate me with romance, but I don't know if they think I was. I was often considered the object, not the one longing, so to speak. I think when people watch my films that's the image they get."

I think about her films. About my father's collection. About *Roman Holiday* that first afternoon with Tobias. The myth, the magic, of this movie star. But Audrey Hepburn isn't Holly Golightly, in the little black dress and trench coat in the rain. She isn't Nicole, in Paris, planning a museum heist and falling in love with the handsome burglar. She isn't Eliza Doolittle, climbing the ranks of society. All that was fiction. Ideas concocted in the minds of studio heads. Audrey Hepburn is simply the woman standing beside me now.

She looks at me curiously, like she's waiting to see if I'll ask it. The reason we're out here together. The reason, perhaps, she's here tonight. Her advice, finally.

"What do I do?" I ask her.

"Do you have a choice?" she says.

I look back inside. I see Tobias.

"I don't know," I say. "I thought I could . . ." I trail off.

Audrey puts her hand on my shoulder. It startles me. Her fingers are light, cool in the night air. They feel like raindrops.

"Sweetheart," she says. "You could not wish me alive."

"I know," I say. "Of course. But Tobias . . . It wasn't supposed to happen like this. We weren't supposed to end like this."

"Maybe," she says. Her hand is still there. I have a feeling that the punch line hasn't been delivered yet—she's trying to soften the blow. "But knowing what *I* do," she says, "having a partner you can exist in the world with, not one who you need to tuck away with, makes life a lot easier." She threads her thumb across my shoulder. "What's done is done."

"No," I say. I have the urge to throw her hand away, to stomp off, to *yell* at Audrey Hepburn. "It was my fault. . . ." All of a sudden I'm crying. Big, hiccuping tears, and Audrey takes me in her arms. She's a tiny woman, of course, all bones, but she still feels nurturing—bigger and softer than her frame.

"What I'm telling you," she whispers, rubbing my back in small circles, "is that it's not your place. You do not get to reignite someone else's life."

"But what about all of this?" I say. "How is this happening? And why?"

"My love," she says. She pulls me back. She holds me at arm's length. "You know why."

"No," I say again. I step back from her, but she holds me steady, and I feel it rising, that tide of water—threatening to carry me out to sea.

"You need to," she says. "You asked me what you do?"

I nod.

"You say good-bye."

TWENTY-THREE

W E DECIDED TO DRIVE INTO Great Barrington the next day and have lunch at this pizza place we heard was great, Baba Louie's. Post-vegetarianism, Tobias had decided to see if the gluten-free lifestyle would suit him (it didn't), and they made a wheat-less crust there. Plus we wanted to enjoy the town—walk around, shop, take advantage of the fresh air and the fact that there wasn't yet snow on the ground. We were still buoyed by the previous night, by the closeness we felt being alone together.

"Do you want to eat or walk around first?" Tobias asked me.

"Eat," I said. We had forgotten breakfast food on our grocery list, and I was starving.

They didn't open until eleven and we got there at ten forty-five. We huddled outside the door, Tobias rubbing his hands up and down my arms even though it wasn't that cold out.

"Should we get coffee?" Tobias asked me.

"Need sustenance," I said. "If we stand here, maybe they'll open sooner." There was no one in sight and the lights weren't on, but I didn't want to miss our window. Tobias laughed, then obliged.

Finally, a stout man in a white apron came out from the back, flipped on the lights, and let us in. We claimed a table by the window that had a stencil of a pizza pie in it. I felt déjà vu come on the moment we sat—the calm, funny memory of being here before, right like this. We'd never been to the Berkshires before together. I'd come once with my mother, when I was a kid, and once while Tobias was gone, with Paul. But I loved it here, I decided. Forget the beach—this was our place. My mind started to sprint. Maybe we'd even change our plans and get married here. I had this image of me at the Wheatleigh, dressed in a pale lilac dress, a flower crown on my head. Summer. Our friends seated in white wooden chairs as I floated down the aisle toward Tobias.

"What are you thinking about?" he asked me. It was something he asked frequently at the beginning of our relationship, almost never anymore. I took this as a sign that he didn't really want to know, but here, now, it felt like salvation.

"That it would be really beautiful to get married here."

He sat back in his chair. It was a sign of withdrawal, but how big I couldn't tell.

"I thought we were doing Park Slope with just the six of us?"

We had decided on: Tobias, me, Jessica, Sumir, Matty, my mom. Tobias didn't want his parents there, so I didn't press. He wasn't particularly close with them, but he never had been.

"I know," I said. "I was just thinking it's really beautiful up here. And there would be room for so many more people we love."

"I thought Park Slope was our compromise," he said. He was a little irritated, a little agitated. "I told you I wanted to elope."

"And I told you I don't," I said. His irritation beckoned a response from me. It was like all I had been burying, suppressing, came rumbling to the surface—a rupture, a fault line.

"Right. That's why we're doing the church."

The waitress came over then. She had large holes in her ears from piercings and purple hair and looked to be about twenty. I wondered if she was in high school or college and whether she lived at home. At that moment, I thought of my dad.

"Are you guys ready to order?" she asked.

We asked for a minute. Maybe we shouldn't have. Maybe we should have ordered our pizza. Maybe she would have brought it at just the exact right time to prevent what happened next.

That's the thing about life—these moments that define us emerge out of nothing. A missed call. A trip down the stairs. A car accident. They happen in a moment, a breath.

"So you want a big wedding?" Tobias asked. It wasn't an accusation, not exactly, but I could hear the bubble of animosity under his question. *A big wedding*. It was like wanting tax cuts for the rich. More than frivolous—a show of privilege that was not only unnecessary and gaudy, but detrimental.

"Yes," I said. "I want a big wedding." I was challenging him. It wasn't even true. I didn't want a big wedding. I didn't even have that many friends and barely any family, but I wanted to expose his mentality to the light. I wanted to point to it and say, *See? This is why we're here. It's not me, it's you.*

"Okay," he said. "Fine. We'll have a big wedding. We'll do it up here. Can we have lunch now?"

It was what I had wanted to hear, but it was all wrong. We were sacrificing ourselves in order to one-up each other.

And then I saw the truth: We didn't know how to make each other happy.

I thought he knew what I needed. That I wanted to believe we were moving forward, that we'd grow up and out of this stage, that we'd build a life together that had some stability—but he didn't. Or maybe he saw it but he couldn't give it to me. All our fights, all our snips and groans and frosty mornings were over this simple fact. He wanted to make me happy, and I wanted him to *be* happy, and the two weren't compatible.

"No," I said. "I don't think we can."

"Jesus, Sabrina, what do you want?"

"I want us to be on the same page. And we're not. We haven't been in a long time."

"So this is my—"

"No," I said. "It's not. It's not anyone's fault. But we do this all the time. We just keep poking and poking and poking each other. We don't want the same things. We have never even talked about kids."

"We haven't even figured out how to get *married*," he said. He ran a hand over his face. "Why can't we ever take one thing at a time?"

"Because we don't. We just stand still, and we resent each other for it." It cut my heart right in two to say it out loud.

He got up and walked outside. I followed him. The sun had moved behind a cloud, and it was freezing. My coat was inside, looped over the back of my chair.

"I hate feeling this way and I hate making you feel this way. It's fucking powerless." He put his hands up to rest on the top of his head. "I'm not sure it's supposed to be this hard."

I felt my world come crashing down. I swear it was like the sun fell straight out of the sky.

"We can't keep doing this to each other," he said. I saw how much pain he was in. I saw the sting in his eyes. "I can't keep doing this to you."

I could feel the desperation in him, and I felt it, too. It began to mix with anger, flooding my fearful veins with rage. "Do it, then," I said. I crossed my arms in front of me. I was shaking. "End it."

"Sabby . . ."

"No," I said. I was seeing stars. I knew the sadness would be too big, too wide—I didn't want to feel it. The anger was shorter. Let me burn there.

He started to cry. "Maybe we just need to take some time apart," he said.

I looked at him, dumbfounded. It felt like he had stabbed me with a sword and taken out my heart and lungs in one clean swipe. I said nothing. I looked down at my hands. On my finger was the ring. The beautiful, sweet, subtle ring. The one that was supposed to carry us through decades, not months. I reached over and with shaking fingers took it off. I couldn't keep it. I couldn't even look at it.

I handed it back to him. "Pawn it," I said, my voice shaking. "You need the money."

I walked back into Baba Louie's, grabbed my coat, and walked out. We went back to the cabin, packed in silence, and then we drove back to the city. I stared out the window, my feet tucked up into my chest on the seat. I was too numb to cry.

"This isn't a breakup," he said. "It's just some time. I just think we need to be alone for a bit. Don't you? Sabby?"

I was scared of being without him, of course I was. But what terrified me more was him being without me—what he would find in that quiet. Whether it would be his happiness.

11:21 P.M.

AUDREY AND I ARE STILL OUTSIDE. I've smoked three cigarettes; she's finishing her second.

"We should return," she says, although neither one of us makes a move. I know that she's right, that it's time to go back inside, because time is almost up, and now that I know what to do, I need to do it.

Conrad appears at the door.

"My dears," he says. "You'll catch cold if you stay much longer."

"Such a gentleman," Audrey demurs. She puts her cigarette out on the window ledge. "Shall we?"

Conrad holds the door open and I follow Audrey inside.

"How was it out there?" Tobias asks. There is a hope in his voice, a childish lilt that makes my heart break, and I know it's there because he thinks there's a way out, that maybe Audrey and I uncovered it in the night air. How am I going to tell him there isn't, that I can't? That life isn't like the movies we loved but something infinitely more complex?

I look to Jessica, but she's still in the bathroom. Robert nurses his coffee.

"I'm sorry," I say to Robert. I'll start there.

He sets down his cup, startled.

"I'm sorry that it didn't work out with Mom, and that you guys lost that baby, and that when you got well you couldn't or didn't come back, and that I never knew you. I'm sorry I didn't try harder to find you when I could, and that when I did, I left and didn't go through with it. I don't know if it would have helped, but I don't want you to feel tortured anymore. I don't think it's helpful for you, nor do I think it's helpful for me. I don't want to carry around your regrets, and I think in some ways that's what happened. I think I picked them up somewhere along the line, maybe to hate you, maybe to feel closer to you, I don't know, but I know they're too heavy for me now, and I have to give them back to you."

Robert sits up straighter. I swear I think he's going to hold out his hands.

"You don't have to carry them, though," I say. "Just because I'm giving them back. You can leave them here."

Robert's eyes well up with tears. "That would be all right," he says.

I stand up from my chair, because I want to hug him. Not to make him feel better, but because I want to feel him. I have no memories of hugging my father. I imagine he held me when I was little, maybe even rocked me to sleep, but he never picked me up off the sidewalk when I scraped my knee or dusted off me after a fall from my bike. He didn't carry me on his shoulders or up the stairs. Didn't tackle me in the backyard during a game of touch football or let me climb onto his feet for a father-daughter dance. And I know I won't get all that back, that there's no way to, that it's lost like the shells of the sea. But I want to feel what it's like to be in his arms, to be loved by him, just once.

"Dad," I say. He seems to know, and he stands up and embraces me. He smells like him, not like I remember, because I don't, but like I expected him to, and this more than anything makes me cry into his shoulder. He puts one hand on my back and the other on my head. I know he's done this many times before, with his girls, and I'm aware of the fact that we only get this one, this shot today. That's it. Maybe it can't make up for anything, but it can prevent some future pain, maybe even precipitate some peace.

He pulls back and holds me at arm's length. "It wasn't easy to do what you just did," he says. "It shows what a strong woman you are. Your mother did well with you."

I kiss his cheek. I wonder if he'll remember this, wherever he goes to next. I think he will. I hope so.

I sit back down. Across the table Audrey and Conrad beam at me, like proud parents.

Jessica comes back to the table. "This thing takes forever when it doesn't have a full charge," she says, dropping the pump back into her bag. "What did I miss?"

Robert smiles at me. He looks stronger than he did earlier tonight, and it makes me feel proud, somehow.

"I think we should get the check," I say.

Next to me, Tobias shifts. "What about us?" he asks.

Conrad pushes back his chair to get the waiter's attention. Audrey's eyes are fixed steadily on me.

I'm reminded of one of Jessica's sayings, a magnet that stuck to our refrigerator for the duration of our time together.

All good things must come to an end.

"Baby," I say. Something I haven't said in so long. I take his hands in my own. Tears are streaming down my face before I even get the words out. "We have to let go. It's time."

TWENTY-FOUR

TOBIAS WENT TO STAY WITH MATTY as soon as we got back from Great Barrington. I didn't want to think about him, about us, about what this break would mean—so I focused on our past. I replayed our relationship like a YouTube montage of a television show's greatest moments. Us on the beach, the towering canvases around us. Our stopped subway car. Eating pasta in bed. Memories stacked and stacked and stacked so high they threatened to topple.

Tobias and I didn't speak much in the two weeks that followed. A few calls here and there. He checked in on me but I didn't know how to respond. *Good, thanks, just lying at the bottom of the ocean.* We texted about functional things—money, shared items. Sometimes we said "I miss you." Most important, we didn't see each other.

I don't think either one of us knew what we were doing. Breaking up for good seemed impossible, but the more time we spent apart, the more deciding to be together seemed equally unlikely. How would we go back to our life, our relationship, our apartment after this? How would we move forward? We were stuck, and we had been for a long time.

When Matty came over to pick up a box of his stuff, I answered the door in a bathrobe. That had been my routine—come home from work, change into bathrobe, watch *How I Met Your Mother* until my eyes stung and I passed out.

"You look like shit," he told me.

"It's in the bedroom," I said. I walked over and picked up the box from the floor. It was filled mostly with clothes and a few kitchen supplies Tobias had asked if he could "borrow." I shoved it at Matty.

"Have you had dinner?" he asked me.

I shook my head.

"Come on," he said. "I'm taking you out."

We didn't go far. A ramen place in my neighborhood the three of us had been to many times together. But it was enough for me to put on jeans, a sweater, and lip gloss.

"You're a vision," Matty said when I emerged.

"Sarcasm was never your strong suit," I told him.

"Who says I'm being sarcastic?"

We ordered bowls at the counter and a bottle of wine. They had a cheap white that always did the trick. Matty poured as I slurped noodles.

"Good?" he asked.

"Better," I said. I couldn't remember the last time I'd had a real meal. My jeans, when I put them on, hung sloppily on my hips.

"He's still with you?" I asked. Tobias hadn't said, but I'd assumed.

Matty nodded. "Yeah. But I have room." He had bought a two-bedroom in Brooklyn Heights. It was far less showy than the Mid-town loft had been. It was a second-floor walk-up with crown molding in an above-average prewar building, and I loved it. Big floor-to-ceiling bay windows on a tree-lined street.

"He's never going to change," I said. I downed my wine. Matty refilled.

"He will," he said. "Everyone does. But, you know, maybe it's wrong to think you guys have to change for each other."

I looked over at him. He had grown up in the time I'd known him. His personality—updated from excited puppy to passionate man—had affected his exterior. He dressed like a grown-up. He was successful. It made me happy for him.

"I don't know," I said.

"You'll figure it out," he said. I was reminded again of the last dinner we'd had just the two of us. I didn't wonder whether he thought *I told you so*. I knew he did.

Matty walked me home and took the small box and loaded it into his car. He gave me a hug. "Be well," he said. "Call me if you need anything."

I went upstairs and dialed Jessica. I hadn't wanted to tell her. In fact, I'd been ducking her calls since Great Barrington. I knew eventually I'd have to. If Tobias hadn't told her already—although I didn't think he would. She'd have tried him when she couldn't reach me, but I didn't think in the current state he'd take her call. I was surprised, in fact, that she was so persistently trying to get ahold of me. She'd been the one doing all the calling.

I pulled a pillow onto my lap and called from the old club chair that used to be ours, and then mine and Tobias's, and I guess was just mine now.

"Hi," she said. "Finally. I thought you were dead."

"No," I said. "I'm here."

"I've been trying to get ahold of you," she said.

"I know, I'm sorry. Jess—"

"Wait. I have some news. I wanted to tell you in person, but I'm starting to show, so . . . I'm pregnant."

I flashed on a moment in our first apartment, huddled over the sink, trying to read a pregnancy test. Hers. She had been with Sumir for years at that point, but we were still only twenty-two, hardly ready for a baby. It was negative, and we squealed, jumping up and down.

Change is the only true constant.

"Amazing!" I said. "I'm happy for you." And I was. I knew she wanted it, as much as I knew anything about Jessica then. Her life in Connecticut eluded me. So much of who she was seemed to have dissipated over time. I felt she still knew me, but only because I was who I had always been—maybe that was unfair, too. "How far along are you?" I asked.

"Four months," she said.

Four months. She had been pregnant the entire fall. August, too.

"How are you?" she asked.

I could have told her then, but I didn't. I told myself it was because I didn't want to tamp down her joy, but it wasn't, at least not entirely. It was because I didn't trust her with this grief. And that made me sad—sadder, possibly, than I even was about Tobias.

"Fine," I said. "You know, work."

"Come out soon," she said. "I'm gonna be so fat in like a second. My pants already don't fit." There was a note of something in her voice . . . was it some kind of longing? Nostalgia? I wanted to believe the tone in her words. *I miss you.*

"I'm sure you're glowing," I said. "And I'd love to come."

"Sab?" Jessica said. She hadn't used my nickname in a long time. "I hope it's not a boy."

I laughed. So did she. It felt good, even over the phone.

"Let's do something next weekend," she said. "Or the one after."

"You got it."

We hung up. Later, after she'd asked me why I hadn't said anything, I'd told her the truth: *I was afraid you'd tell me it was for the best.*

11:32 P.M.

IN RESPONSE TO MY SUGGESTION of good-bye, Tobias pushes back his chair and stands up. He doesn't say anything, just walks over to the window. Conrad raises his eyebrow at me, but Jessica is already up. She follows Tobias over to the window and they stand next to each other. I find Audrey's eyes across the table. They tell me to stay put, and so I do.

I don't much feel like talking. The others linger in silence now. The waiter is clearing our last remaining plates. Audrey is asking for some more water. He hands me the check, and despite Conrad's protestations I give my credit card. I want to pay. It's my dinner party, after all.

I look up at the clock. The second hand ticks steadily, like a soldier marching into war. I have a memory, like the flash of a camera, of my father singing to me when I was a baby, stomping around the kitchen.

I left my wife and forty-eight children alone in the kitchen in starving condition with nothing to eat but gingerbread. Left. Left. Left, right, left.

It's not until I hear my father that I realize I'm singing out loud. He starts in with me. *Left. Left. Left, right, left.*

Then Conrad joins in. His big, bellowing voice fills the restaurant, and I'm glad we're alone at this point, save the dish washers and our waiter. Audrey pipes in, too, and the four of us chant on together.

"This is an awful nursery rhyme when you think about it," Audrey says, breaking out of rhythm.

"Particularly for me," Robert says. "Although I do fondly remember teaching it to you."

"They all are," Conrad says. "'Mary, Mary, Quite Contrary' is about the homicidal nature of Queen Mary."

"And the one with the well," Audrey says.

"The well?" Conrad says. "I'm not aware of one about a well."

Audrey frowns. "I feel a little unsteady," she says. "Must be all the wine." She glances up at the clock on the wall, and I feel something squeeze in my stomach. I look over at Jessica and Tobias. *There's no time, there's no time, there's no time.*

I can't stand it any longer. I stand up and walk over to them.

"How's it going over here?" I ask.

Jessica looks at Tobias. "Well, he's dead, and it appears he's going to remain that way, so not great."

Tobias starts to laugh then. It's been so long since I've heard his laugh. Longer, by far, than the time he's been gone.

Jessica puts her hand on my shoulder. "I'm still here," she says.

"We'll work it out, we have the time." She squeezes my shoulder, taps Tobias on the chest, and goes back to the table.

"I wish I could take you away from here," he says. He's looking out the window, not at me. At the passing taxis and a few lingering people on the sidewalk. Outside the city spins, unaware.

"Where would we go?" I ask.

"Maybe down to the West Side Highway," he says. "We could walk along the water."

"Not far enough," I say. I go to stand shoulder to shoulder with him.

"You're right. We never got to go to Mexico, or Paris, or Guam," he says. "I regret that."

"Don't," I say. "No more regrets."

I put my head on his shoulder.

"What's going to happen to me now?" he asks. I turn to look at him, and I see the fear dancing just around the perimeter.

"I don't know," I say. "I wish I did. I don't think you'll be where you were, though. I think you'll be . . ." My voice catches, and in the space he answers.

"Gone," he says.

My cheeks are wet. I haven't stopped crying. "There isn't any more time."

He nods. His eyes are wet, too. "I'm so sorry," he says. "We were so good at being together but so bad at the rest of it."

"The rest of it was important," I say. "I think more than we realized."

He nods. "Were we always going to end up here?" he asks.

I think about the decade we spanned, the entirety of it splayed out before us tonight.

"I don't know," I say. "But we did. I think that's what matters now."

He takes my face in his hands. "I love you," he says. "Always."

Meant to be. I used to think that about us. That we were meant to be. That the stars had aligned to bring us together. It never occurred to me that our fate might not be forever.

TWENTY-FIVE

I T HAPPENED ON A SATURDAY. I was at home, doing laundry. I
had planned to head out to Jessica's in the afternoon. We were going
to go to an early dinner, since she said she was now getting tired at
seven. I was going to see her belly. I hadn't seen Tobias since the day
he dropped me off nearly a month ago.

It was early December now, and we were creeping into winter.
Christmas lights were strung around the city. The window displays
were up at Bloomingdale's, Bergdorf's, and Barneys. Going up and
seeing them was something Jessica and I used to do together. We'd
get hot chocolates at Serendipity on Third Avenue and then make our
way through the city, hitting all the big department stores. Sometimes we even made it all the way down to Lord and Taylor. We never
made it inside the stores; we were broke anyway. It was just to look at

the windows—the spinning displays of confetti silver and gold, life-sized candy canes, winter wonderland scapes.

I was folding one of Tobias's shirts when I heard it. It was an old UCLA one, soft cotton, that I'd taken to sleeping in. He hadn't taken it, and when Matty came for more clothes I purposefully left it out.

I heard the screech of tires and the crunch of metal and the shattering of glass through my closed window. I ran to it and looked down into the street. Someone had been hit, that much was clear. People were outside shouting. I grabbed a down vest off my bed and ran down into the street.

I was barely out my front door when I saw him. Just a leg, to the right of the car. It was his shoe, though. This old pair of Dr. Martens with the soles worn in. I would have recognized them anywhere. I ran.

His body was half under the car. Later the driver would argue that he had come out of nowhere, that he had practically run into the street. But now his body was mangled. His shoulder was crushed, his leg bent at an impossible angle.

"Call nine-one-one!" I screamed. I bent down next to him. His body was warm. I could smell him, those cigarettes and that honey. I put my hands on his head and held them there. "It's okay, it's okay," I whispered over and over again. I bent my head down low to his mouth to check, to see where the air was. I couldn't find it. It's strange the tricks adrenaline plays on you. The need to fix, to rectify. In the moment of impact we think it's possible to go back. We're so close to the previous minute; how hard would it be to just turn back the clock? To just quickly undo what has just been done?

I stayed that way, my face pressed to his, until the paramedics arrived. Getting him unhooked from underneath the car was complicated, and more than once they tore at his limbs further, but I didn't look away. I had the feeling that if my eyes left his, even for a moment, he'd be gone. That the only thing keeping him there was the fact that I was, too. *Please. Stay with me.*

I rode with him in the ambulance. I must have called Jessica at some point, although I do not remember that. I remember him being rushed into the operating room. And I remember her being there, hours later, when the doctor came out. *I'm sorry. We tried. Too much damage.*

He never woke up.

Jessica started to cry next to me, but I felt blank. Like an empty white room with no trace of a door. I wanted to see him, but they told me I couldn't. *Family only.* But I *was* family. We had been together for nine years. I was the only family he had, and he needed me. Even if he was no longer there.

"We have to call his parents," Jessica said. All I knew about them was that they lived in Ohio and had once taken us to an Olive Garden in Times Square.

I sat down in the hospital waiting room. I didn't want to leave. Where would I go?

I found their number in my phone. His mom answered on the third ring. I counted. I told her there'd been an accident. She kept saying she was sorry, like I was the one who had lost something. Maybe that was her defense, to believe I had lost more, that I could shoulder more of the burden. I found out later he'd never told her we were taking time apart.

She said they would get on the next flight out. We would need to plan a funeral, she guessed. She choked on the word. Did I know where we could get some flowers?

They gave me his effects on the way out. A plastic bag, zip locked at the top. I couldn't bring myself to open it.

"We need to go," Jessica said.

"No," I said. "We can't. We can't leave him." I started to scream it, the sobs tearing through my body. "We can't leave."

Jessica held me, her pregnant belly between us. "Okay," she said. "We'll stay."

We sat in that hospital waiting room until three o'clock in the morning. Jessica took me home and stayed with me until Tobias's parents arrived the next day. When I saw his father I broke down again.

The last thing Tobias had ever said to me was over the phone. "Do you know what my T-Mobile password is? I need to change my plan."

I told him I'd see if I had it in my password folder and I'd text if I did.

"Sabby?" he'd asked.

"Yes?"

"Five."

"Tired," I'd said, and hung up.

11:47 P.M.

TOBIAS AND I GO BACK TO the table. Audrey is becoming fidgety. My father looks tired. Conrad is yawning, tapping his breastbone like he's readying to curl up by the fire with a scotch and close his eyes.

"Thank you all," I say. "I have no idea how this came to be, but I'm glad it did. I hope it's real."

"It's real," Jessica says. "My boobs don't lie." She points to her milk-crusted shirt. "Plus," she says. "Why wouldn't it be?"

I feel my heart pull toward her, Jessica Bedi, my best friend. Somewhere deep in there, below the trappings of her life, is a woman who still believes in magic.

Anything is possible.

"I dare say it is," Conrad says. "I feel a slight hangover coming on."

"I don't suppose you'll have to find your way back," Audrey asks him. She seems, all at once, concerned.

"Perhaps," Conrad says. "But I know how to hail a taxi."

I look around the table. This dinner began as a reminder of all I had lost, but as I watch them now all I can feel is profoundly grateful. For a father who never stopped loving me, for a movie star who gave a generation her grace and who gave us one dinner tonight, for a professor who challenges his students, and for a best friend who is still here.

"Thank you," I say.

Conrad nods; Jessica clears her throat. Across the table, Audrey blows me the most delicate of kisses.

"Well, shall we?" Audrey asks. "It's about that time."

I look up at the clock. Twelve minutes to midnight.

"How should we do this?" I ask the group.

Conrad claps his hands together. "I'll go first," he says. He pushes back his chair and stands up, adjusting his suit jacket. "I expect a lengthy e-mail and perhaps a telephone call this week. I'll wait for it."

"You can count on it. Thank you for being here," I tell him. "We needed you."

He turns his attention to Audrey, who doesn't seem to know whether to remain sitting or to stand. Conrad takes her hand. "It has been my supreme pleasure, Ms. Hepburn," he says, kissing it gently.

"Oh," she says. "Oh."

Conrad shakes Robert's hand, pats Tobias on the back, and gives us a little salute. He walks out the door. I follow his silhouette until it is lost down the street.

Next it's Audrey. She stands and loops her little Chanel sweater over her shoulders. "It's gotten chilly outside," she says. She seems nervous now, without Conrad, and I feel a wave of affection for her, that she stuck this out until the very end.

"It has been an honor to spend the evening with you," my father says. He stands with her. "I'll walk you out."

He looks back at me, and I want to tell him I'm not ready, that this should be the start, not the end. But our time is up.

"I'm thankful I got to know you tonight, Sabrina," he says. "I'd say I'm proud, but I hardly feel responsible."

"Say it anyway," I tell him.

He comes over to me. He leans down so he's right next to my ear. "My daughter," he says, like he's savoring the word.

He kisses me on the cheek, and then he's gone with Audrey, out the door in the night air.

"And then there were three," Jessica says.

"It's always been a crowd," Tobias says.

Jessica smiles. "I'll go," she says. She looks at her watch. "The baby will be up in forty-five minutes. Maybe I'll make the feeding." She slings her bag over her shoulder. "I'll call you later," she says. "Okay?"

"Yeah. Hey, Jess?"

"Uh-huh?"

"Thank you for coming tonight."

"It's our tradition, right?" she says. "Although next year is in trouble. I'm not exactly sure we can keep this one up." She turns to Tobias. "Be good, okay?" She puts a hand on his arm. I see her eyes well up with tears.

"I got nowhere to go but up." It's a joke, but none of us laughs.

"I'll see you," she says, and leaves, the bells on the door jingling after her.

We're alone.

Tobias turns toward me. "Should we walk a bit?" he asks.

I look at the clock. We have six minutes left.

"Yeah," I say.

We put on our coats. Tobias holds the door open for me as we stroll out into the night. The white wicker bench is there, perched by the door. I wish we could sit on it, even for just five minutes more.

"I'll walk you back," he says.

"We won't make it," I say.

"Even so," he says, and we head toward home.

TWENTY-SIX

I T TOOK ME A WEEK TO open the personal effects bag the hospital gave me.

We had the funeral on a Sunday, at the church in Park Slope where we were supposed to be married. Tobias's parents picked up bagels and Jessica wrote and read a poem. We all wore color because I thought it's what you do when you're not trying to be somber, when you're trying to celebrate life. But I was mourning. I was wearing a red dress, one Tobias had liked, but inside I felt black.

Matty came and sat next to me, and then after we walked the city for twelve hours, barely speaking. He seemed to understand that there were no words to make it livable and didn't bother trying. We were together in that grief, and that was something. I was grateful for that. To be with someone else who had really known him.

Afterward I sat on the floor of our bedroom and slid the manila envelope out of the plastic wrapping. I took a breath in and held it, like I was preparing to go underwater. Inside was his cell phone, wallet, a subway card, and a ring box. I opened it immediately. It was not the ring I'd given him back but the other one, the first one we'd seen. The one we fought over, that was too expensive. He'd gone back and bought it.

The thought that still felt too hot to think, like if I gave it any time it would burn me alive, was what he was doing on my street corner. *He came running out of nowhere*, the driver had said.

He was running to me. And now, I knew, he was running across with this ring in his pocket. It could only mean one thing: he had come to get me. Our time apart had come to an end just as he'd decided he wanted us to be together.

My heart seized. I thought surely I'd die right along with him. In that moment, I wanted to. Because the alternative was just too cruel. To know, so clearly, that he was coming back to make it work. That he had saved up, presumably, over our time apart and bought this ring, the first we'd seen, to make a new promise, a bigger one—I didn't know how to live with that.

The ring was beautiful, just as I'd remembered. I slipped it out of its black velvet seat and put it on my hand. It fit perfectly. It was dazzling—it picked up the afternoon light and sent it cascading everywhere—on the wooden floor below me, off the white walls. "It's beautiful," I said out loud.

I couldn't explain why, in that moment, I thought about the old ring and what had happened to it. Had he brought it back to Ingrid and traded it in? Did he pawn it? Was it still somewhere buried underneath his stuff? Matty hadn't gone through his things yet. We said we'd do it together, but I didn't know when either of us would be ready, or if we ever would be. The thought of folding his jeans, taking down his shirts, sifting through his photos? Impossible.

I wore the ring all day, and then I put it back in its box and hid it under my bed where his photograph used to be.

12:00 A.M.

T OBIAS STOPS. NEITHER ONE OF US has said anything for a minute, and now here it is, upon us.

"Well," he says. We haven't yet made it home, but there's one thing I have left to ask. It's the question I've been waiting to ask him all night, since we first arrived at this dinner nearly four hours ago. It's the only one left. But of course I know, don't I? Even so, I need to hear him say it.

"Why were you there that day?"

He exhales and nods, like he knew it was coming, of course he did. "I was going to re-propose," he says. "Set a date. Call our parents. Have a *big* wedding." He smiles and lets out a small laugh. "I wanted the right ring."

I think about the fight we had that day in the store. The way his pride was damaged. "It's a beautiful ring," I say.

His features are lit up in the moonlight, and I see him as that nineteen-year-old kid on the beach in Santa Monica. Beautiful and stubborn with everything ahead of him. "It wasn't the right one, though," he says. "I was still getting it wrong. The one we picked out together? That was ours."

"Yes," I say.

"You were the great love of my life," he says. "That's just how it happened. But I won't be yours." He isn't sad, not even a little bit. "I don't want to be."

"Tobias," I say. I feel my eyes sting up again.

"Not forever. Okay?"

I nod. "Okay."

"Here," he says. "I want you to have this." He hands me the pocket watch, the one that was my father's, that I gave him.

"It was a gift," I say.

"Still is," he tells me. "Like Robert said—I can't take it with me."

Tobias wraps his arms around me. I drop my face into his neck, but then I open my eyes, because I don't want to miss seeing him, not a moment of him.

"I didn't tell you," he says. "I remember now."

I look up at him. "What?"

He pauses, like he's taking me in. His eyes drift over my face like it's a lazy Sunday afternoon. Like we have all the time in the world in which to gaze.

"You were wearing a red tank top and denim shorts. Your hair was down and you kept swinging your arms by your sides. I thought you were going to knock someone over."

I think about the two of us, standing in the sand, no idea how entwined our lives were already—and would be.

"That's how I see you," he says. He gives me a little salute, and then he's gone.

Just like that. He doesn't so much disappear as he leaves. I imagine he's off to the corner deli, picking up cigarettes and a bottle of off-brand seltzer.

I walk the rest of the way home alone. I find my keys at the bottom of my bag by an old piece of dried-out gum and a lip gloss. I climb the stairs to my apartment. It's dark, and I flip on a light. There are remnants of birthday cake on the counter, and I drop my bag down next to them—a slice of frosting, chocolate crumbs. I head into the bedroom.

I take the shoebox out from under my bed and rifle though it—photos of Tobias and me, keys to our old apartment, Broadway Playbills, movie stubs, the wrinkled Post-it, the ring—until I find what I'm looking for. It's a letter, addressed to me, from Alex Nielson, dated 2006. I open it and read.

Dear Sabrina,

It's strange to be writing you this, although I suppose stranger for you to be reading it. My name is Alex and I'm your sister. We share a father, Robert Nielson, who gave me your name, and I looked you up. It's really cool that you're at USC. I'd love to go there someday, although I'm not sure I'll get in. I'm only in eighth grade but my grades aren't very good. I love to write though.

I'm the older of two. I have a younger sister, Daisy. We don't really get along. Sometimes that makes me wonder if you and I would and other times it makes me convinced I have to know you. I guess that's why I'm writing.

Dad talks about you. Not a lot, but sometimes. When I ask he always will. He told me that he hasn't seen you since you were a little girl. He said he doesn't want to disturb the life you have now and I understand but I also sometimes wish he would. He's a good dad. It makes me sad to think you don't know that.

He told me a story about you the other day. Daisy was carrying on about her name. She doesn't like it. She thinks it's too girly. She's all goth right now—total rocker chick. She asked why they gave her that name and my mom (her name is Jeanette) said it was because daisies were the first thing she saw in the hospital room when she had her. Daisy thinks that's lame. Anyway after dinner I asked about you. I wanted to know why they named you Sabrina. Is that strange? I've never even met you before. All I've seen are photos of you when you were very small.

He told me he loved Audrey Hepburn. He said she was his favorite actress. On his first date with your mom he took her to see Sabrina. It was playing at a black-and-white theater and they got popcorn and milk duds—this is all him, btw. He told me the details. Sabrina was his favorite of Audrey's movies. He thought it meant something that the heroine isn't a shrinking violet—that she goes in search of a life for herself and returns stronger for it. He told me when he met you he thought that's the kind of woman you'd be.

I bet he was right.

Love,

Alex

P.S. If you'd ever like to get together let me know. Dad promised to take me to an exhibit in Santa Monica next week. It's on the beach. Maybe we could meet there.

There are many ways stories can unfold, and now I see this one begin to take shape. Something different in the space where there used to be just the one thing. I put the watch and receipt in the box, proof of the night, of the decade—of what was once and is no longer—but when I go to close it the lid won't fit. There is something stuck up against the side. I let my fingers thread in between the cardboard until they find the foreign object. I unhook it and hold it in my hands, and that's when I see it's the photograph. Not Tobias's, not the one I lost, but the one we stood in front of on the beach that first day. The little boy and the eagle. It's a print no bigger than a postcard.

I never bought it, I'm sure of that. But here it is in the effects box. The little boy stands with wings spread out behind him, his eyes closed. He appears just as he was that day ten years ago—to be soaring.

I take out a pen. I flip the photo over. I think about what comes after—how much there is to say. Twenty-four years. Birthdays. Cross-country moves. Jobs and life. *Begin*, I think. *Begin begin begin*.

Dear Alex, I write. And for the first time in a long time I know exactly what it is I want to say.

Acknowledgments

To James Melia, my brilliant editor, who gave me a soft place to land when I really needed it and made the process of this book so wonderfully delightful. Thank you for loving these characters as I do.

To Erin Malone, my incredible literary agent, for being the toughest editor and greatest champion. I didn't think I'd ever find you. Thank god I did. Also: You're never getting rid of me.

To Dan Farah, my miraculous manager. You make everything I do bigger, better. This road is brutal and beautiful. Thank you for hanging in with me. I love you.

To everyone at Flatiron Books, especially Bob Miller, Amy Einhorn, and Marlena Bittner for being the most loving, warm, dynamic, and exciting place for Sabrina. You guys rock.

To David Stone, my television agent, for his steadfast belief and Jedi skills. Thanks for being our grown-up.

To Laura Bonner, Caitlin Mahoney, and Matilda Forbes Watson for ensuring this book travels far and wide.

To Leila Sales, Lexa Hillyer, Jessica Rothenberg, and Lauren Oliver for their endless encouragement, love, and life talks. What would I be without this community we've created?

To Jen Smith, for being the best adult sherpa in town. I adore you.

To Melissa Seligmann, for letting me play with our past and for pushing me to honor our present.

To Hannah Gordon, BFF and first reader. I continue to be so screwed without you.

To Raquel Johnson, for fielding every phone call and loving me with such incredible blindness. Baby, we are so lucky.

To Chris Fife and Bill Brown, who saw me through one of the toughest years of my life with extraordinary compassion. You are my angels.

To the cast of *Famous in Love*, who made me a mama for the very first time—never in my wildest dreams did I think I'd get so lucky.

To my parents, who remain my true north. It's a good thing I've been single for so long—otherwise I'd have nothing to write about. You have done your job so remarkably well.

And finally, to any woman who has ever felt betrayed by fate or love. Hang in there. This isn't the end of your story.

The Dinner List

by Rebecca Serle

1. Once Sabrina arrives at the dinner and is greeted by everyone, she thinks, "I didn't really think this through. When I chose each of these five people to be on my list, it was entirely about me. I didn't think how they'd get along together." Why do you think Sabrina chose the people she did, and how do they all play their part as the evening progresses?

2. *The Dinner List* has been called a romantic comedy by reviewers and critics. How does Rebecca Serle both meet the expectations of a romantic comedy and also subvert them?

3. Rebecca doesn't explain the magic of why the dinner takes place; it just simply does for Sabrina. Did you appreciate this choice or would you have liked a bit more explanation? Why do you think Sabrina had this magical dinner?

4. Were you surprised about what happened to Tobias? How does the novel change once this is revealed?

5. Did you end up marrying the first love of your life?

6. How does the dinner help Sabrina heal her relationship with Jessica?

7. Rebecca uses the dinner as a framework to explore Sabrina's tumultuous twenties. How does this unique structure help to add tension? Were there any twists that took you by surprise?

8. What do you think the novel ultimately has to say about love? What do you think it has to say about family?

9. Why do you think the author chose Audrey Hepburn as her celebrity guest?

10. This final one is easy: Who would be on your dinner list?